"721 Montague Street"

The
Strange Doings
of
J. Leslie Ryder

a Sherlock Holmes story

BY DANIEL GRACELY

GRANDMA'S ATTIC PRESS
2002

I want to thank my wife, Alison, and my long-time friend, Jim Rhynard, for their editing help. My conversations with another friend, Andrew Steiger has been an encouragement. Finally, special thanks go again to my brother, David, for his continued help, ideas, and shared enthusiasm.

THIS BOOK IS A WORK OF FICTION. THE CHARACTERS IN THIS STORY ARE FICTIONAL. ANY RESEMBLANCE TO PERSONS LIVING OR DEAD IS PURELY COINCIDENTAL. IT IS A FACT OF HISTORY, HOWEVER, THAT THE MOSA LISA WAS STOLEN FROM THE LOUVRE MUSEUM IN AUGUST 1911. ALSO, THE MOST IMPORTANT AND INTRODUCTORY MODERN ART EXHIBIT IN AMERICA, GENERALLY KNOWN AS THE NEW YORK ARMORY SHOW, OCCURRED IN 1913.

THE STRANGE DOINGS OF J. LESLIE RYDER:
(a Sherlock Holmes story)
Copyright 2002 Daniel D. Gracely
First published by Grandma's Attic Press
November, 2002

Illustrations by Sidney Paget

"Watson won't allow that I know anything of art, but that is mere jealously because our views upon the subject differ."

—Sherlock Holmes to Sir Henry Baskerville
Chapter XIII, *The Hound of the Baskervilles*

Chapter One

It was a cold and blustery April day nearly eight months after the infamous theft of the *Mona Lisa* from the Louvre Museum in Paris, when Sherlock Holmes, some two-hundred miles away in his apartment at Baker Street, stretched out his legs before the fire. It had been a week of frustration for him. The Reverend Kowell's missing last will and testament was believed hidden in an ancient wood-carved pulpit that had been stolen from a nearby parish, but Holmes had had no success in finding it. Now his client no longer wanted his services, and so Holmes and the refined and heightened senses of his cat-like temperament had to abruptly yield to inactivity.

As he had grown older, however, I noticed that my friend sometimes tolerated such circumstances by eventually forcing his mind into some area of thought wholly different from the case at hand. Yet despite our long association, I found it impossible to anticipate what new interest would next occupy him. In the past I had found Holmes engrossed in a variety of subjects—analyzing the daring chromaticism in Guido's music, for example, deciphering a medieval document from a Turkish monastery, or playing three-dimensional inverted solitaire. I waited patiently one morning, then, as Holmes recalled the final impasse that had thwarted him in the Nguyen-Kowell testament dispute. For an hour he paced the room and spoke of the various contradictions that the evidence had presented. Finally he shrugged his shoulders, dropped them with a sigh, and fingered his pipe briefly before abandoning it to retrieve his violin case from the corner of the room.

Although Holmes's violin playing hardly qualified as a new diversion, I reclined in my chair in anticipation of the happy airs and mournful strains that characterized these musical soliloquies. I had always found that his playing revealed a greater depth to his feelings than otherwise, for his emotions tended to lay dormant beneath layers of indifference. This morning proved no exception. The mask was boldly down, and he freely indulged himself with his own transcriptions of French barcaroles. Gone for the moment was that cold relentless logic of Holmes the thinker, as he submitted his machine-like thoughts to that rarely seen bohemian and artistic side of his personality. Afternoon wore into evening and still the subtle music of Fauré and Massenet wafted through the apartment in sweet, poignant tones. Never, in fact, could I remember a more soulful excursion by Holmes, and not until eight o'clock that evening did it explain itself.

At a quarter before that hour Holmes returned the violin to its case and carefully replaced the bow in its holder. He settled back in his armchair with his left hand turned upward, his fingers opening and closing rapidly in imaginary scales, his gaze fixed deep into the fireplace.

"You are a most inestimable friend, Watson," said he.

"Thank you, Holmes," I said, startled at his uncharacteristic frankness.

"I have, however, an older friend than yourself."

I could not imagine who it might be, for Holmes was solitary in his habits. "I would like to meet him," said I.

"You have been listening to him all day."

"What? Do you mean yourself, Holmes?"

"No, Watson," said he, chuckling. "I mean the violin. I have literally picked out my own violins since my last year at the university."

"Oh," I exclaimed, "have you had this one long? It gives a rich sound, and I imagine the model is rare. I have often wondered if some unique story lay behind your purchase of it."

"Actually I did not purchase it."

"A gift then?"

"In a manner of speaking, I suppose. I picked it from some obliging person's rubbish."

"Great Scott!"

"Yes, I often supported myself at the university by picking through rubbish. My first violin was an excellent find and caused me to write a monograph."

"About the particular model you found, or about violins in general?"

"No, no, the monograph was about rubbish picking! I addressed all the main obstacles: personal esteem, irregularity of trash profile in moonlight, constabulary avoidance, systematizing routes, pawn shop versus the auctioneer, et cetera."

"My dear Holmes!"

"Of course, the art of observation is essential in the rubbish pick. No other activity besides detection requires such keen observation. In fact, one could say that rubbish picking is merely another avenue for detection, and many of the skills necessary for my consulting practice were refined during those midnight hours. My current habit for occasional all-night sittings is itself a carryover from those former days. Yes," concluded Holmes with a twinkle in his eye, "some men have been explorers to the frozen tundra of polar regions, and others to the deepest reaches of sub-continents. I myself was just a frontiersman to the rubbish pile. This instrument in my hand was the *coup de grace* after it was repaired, and even more valuable than the one I found years earlier which nearly caused me to stop rubbish picking altogether."

"Why was that?"

"It was near the end of my university days when I found that first violin, and I began practicing long hours on it, re-acquainting myself with the instrument and flirting with the idea of becoming a symphony player. But I was also planning a private consulting career. Of course, you know which vocation won out. Incidentally, I am expecting a visitor soon, and hope you can remain, as this appointment promises to wed my two loves of rubbish picking and detection. I may lose an old friend in the process, however. Ah, that must be our visitor's step upon the stair."

In a moment a beautiful young woman entered the room, and in the short time it took Holmes to take her coat and motion her into a chair I found myself favorably impressed. She had striking features and a queenly deportment more mature than her years should have yielded. Her appearance, too, was filled with feminine nuance. The whole of her earthen-brown hair fell in cascades past the top of her shoulders in an appearance of calculated disarray, and her rich, soft hair glowed as it hung suspended above the rest of her tall, graceful figure. Her dress, with its sophisticated interplay of material, texture, and olive-brown and red colours, also complimented her bearing, so that the whole effect of Miss Rachel Ann Ryder completely dispelled her age of twenty-three years.

"I'm so sorry, Mr. Holmes, but I decided I must come at once to see you," said she with an upturned face. "I see you are engaged, however."

"This is not a client, Miss Ryder, but my friend, Dr. Watson. Besides, it would not be my habit to see more than one client at a time."

The woman's brow furrowed and she sat forward with a puzzled look on her pretty features.

"Your powers are far beyond anything I have read about, Mr. Holmes. How on earth do you know my name?"

"I recognized your surname in the newspaper as that of a past associate."

"But there was no photograph accompanying my name. And how did you know I was coming?"

"Was it not my telegram that brought you here?" queried Holmes.

"No. I have been at my Aunt Mary's all week."

Holmes gave a look of complete amazement.

"Watson, I cannot remember a more remarkable coincidence. Miss Ryder has arrived at the very hour I requested, but without any knowledge of my communiqué. You credit me with too much, then, Miss Ryder. I only knew your name because I was expecting you. But evidently you have come here for reasons of your own."

"I'm not even sure my coming is justified, Mr. Holmes," she said as the fingers of her hand played nervously with her necklace. "And I'm too curious not to wonder why such a famous detective would want to see *me*."

"I saw the article in the *Times* about your art scholarship at Cambridge. I contacted you because Dr. Watson and I are leaving for America the day after tomorrow, and I wanted to clear up one affair before I went. I own something that once belonged to your father. I shall give it back to your keeping, or, if you prefer, I will make compensation for it."

"My father, Mr. Holmes?" I have not seen my father in twelve years. And you own something of his?"

"This," said my friend, lifting his violin in one hand and the bow in the other. "It is a beautiful instrument. It had been thrown out with the rubbish when I spotted it years ago. Halloa! Hold on, then!"

Our visitor had suddenly grown faint and had slumped down in her seat.

"Some salts, Watson! Steady now—ah, that's better. What do we give ladies? Tea? Very good, Watson! If you please!"

Not until our visitor revived and sipped some Lourdes of Bombay did the colour in her face begin to improve. After some minutes Miss Ryder raised her limp figure in the chair. "I'm fine now, thank you." Her hands still trembled around the teacup as I poured out more of the hot liquid. "Then the violin has survived all these years," commented she in a weak voice. "Mr. Holmes. I do not wish to appear ungrateful, but my artistic ability is not in the direction of music. It would be more practical if you kept the instrument for yourself."

"Then I will make some compensation."

"No, please." The woman grew quiet and tried to steady her nerves. Finally she yielded to my friend's keen gaze of scrutiny. "The truth is, Mr. Holmes, I threw out the violin when I was a young girl. I had grown old enough to understand my mother's hurt over my father's abandonment. One day in anger I smashed my father's violin. Why should it have refuge at my hands when its owner thought little enough to shelter his own daughter? That is how I saw it. Even my Uncle Walter thought so, too."

"And who is Uncle Walter?"

"He is my mother's brother. He came to live with us shortly after my father left us. I grew close to him, but then suddenly he left, too, after only several years. Mother always said that Father was selfish for leaving, but never explained to me why Uncle Walter left. I don't even think she knows where either of them is. My mother always did her best, but we always had one trouble after another after my father deserted us. In the end my mother's spirit collapsed. It seemed she had lost her strength for everything—everything but bitterness, I mean— for I'll never forget the night I found a stack of Bible pages cut from the cover and thrown out onto the rubbish pile."

"How interesting," said Holmes, rubbing his hands. And there was enough light during the night to see this?"

"Yes, it was the clearest and brightest of nights. Some instinct made me pick up the pages and turn them over for a better look. The discovery made a horrible impression on my mind."

"What else did you find besides these pages?"

"Nothing. Except that the stack of pages were thrown on top of some rotted firewood."

"Along with the cover to the Bible, no doubt?"

"No, Mr. Holmes, there was nothing else."

"You are sure about that?" asked Holmes as he leaned forward in his chair.

"Yes."

"How remarkable. And do you remember anything gleaming or glinting in the moonlight as you investigated your find?"

"No—not that I recall."

"Ah! That is suggestive. But go on, Miss Ryder."

"I, too, became melancholy like my mother, and for years I adopted a cynical attitude toward life. Only recently have I forgiven my father and uncle for leaving us, but I am not over-anxious to have an object, such as this violin, remind me of my emotions of that wretched time."

"But even the sale of it would now supplement your scholarship at Cambridge."

"My needs are taken care of, Mr. Holmes."

"You have a sponsor, then?"

The woman briefly looked away. "I've offered to do the laundry and linens for a professor's family. I receive a room in exchange. I don't deny having certain needs, but I won't accept charity."

"Nevertheless," replied my friend, "the highest of three appraisals puts the violin at six pounds fifty—not a princely sum, perhaps, but enough to warrant this draft in your name. With your objection, then," said he with a faint smile as he rose and put the cheque in the pocket of her coat which hung upon the stand.

"I feel most uncomfortable with your doing that, Mr. Holmes," said she.

"A figure twenty times that would be no impropriety, Miss Ryder. It is a small compensation for my having ruined your life."

"What, Mr. Holmes?" she exclaimed with a startled look.

"Not that I intended to. But I think it best to make some financial return as a token of my regret. The upside to all this is that your university expenses are at least provided for."

"I'm afraid I don't understand."

Holmes paused. "Unfortunately, a further explanation of the matter would cast your father in a poor light, Miss Ryder."

"I doubt a worse light, Mr. Holmes, than those shadows of the mind in which I have often held him," she replied

This thought seemed to strike my companion, and after a pause Holmes made a silent appeal to me, and I nodded in return.

"Very well, then, I will tell you the story of the Blue Carbuncle, Miss Ryder. I hope you will not feel afterward that ignorance would have been bliss. But you are of age." Holmes scraped the cold ashes from the bowl of his pipe onto the newspaper at his feet, refilled his pipe with tobacco, and reached into the fire with a pair of tongs. "I once investigated your father, James Ryder, long ago," said he, lighting his pipe with a burning coal. "The good doctor, here, published the story of that event several years ago, though I had never read it until Tuesday last. What prompted me to read Watson's tale was an article about you in Monday's paper. I deduced that your father was the same Ryder whom I had known, and I wanted to refresh my memory of the case. I will follow Dr. Watson's outline in telling it to you and add a few memories of my own. But I will give you a considerable abridgement, for although details in a case are often important, most of

Watson's minutia is superfluous to the story and may be skipped."

"I'm not familiar with the case, Mr. Holmes, but am interested in hearing it. There are gaps in my father's life I would like to know about."

Holmes put his fingertips together and fixed his eyes upon the ceiling.

"Very good, then," he said. *"The Adventure of the Blue Carbuncle,* as Dr. Watson romantically calls it, involved your father, and came to my attention some thirteen years ago around Christmastime. It began one evening when a constable of my acquaintance called on me in an excitable state. He had been on duty the night before when he heard a scuffle at the end of a street and hurried to scatter some ruffians away. By the time he reached the corner the persons had fled, and in their wake one of them had dropped a Christmas goose. There seemed no way to return the bird to its owner, so the constable took it home to his wife to have it prepared for the morrow's dinner. When cleaning the bird, however, she was astonished to find a jewel in its belly. The constable brought it to me, and I recognized it as that unique find from the Amoy River in China, the Blue Carbuncle. It had recently been stolen from the Countess of Morcar. After some little difficulty I traced the crime to your father, James Ryder."

"My father, Mr. Holmes?" Darkness passed over the young woman's face.

"Yes. Your father worked as the head attendant at The Cosmopolitan Hotel where the Countess of Morcar was staying. He and the ladyship's waiting-maid conspired to steal the gem from the Countess during her stay in London. They waited for a convenient time when she was out at the Strand. The maid knew of a plumber who had once been arrested for a minor theft, and one day your father called him to the hotel to fix a leaky water pipe in the Countess's room that she and your father had secretly sabotaged. Later that day the Countess discovered the carbuncle missing and notified the police. They made an immediate investigation, and the result was the arrest of the plumber."

"How horrible, Mr. Holmes!"

"Your father was not accused by the police in that afternoon's investigation, but no gem was found on Horner, and your father feared that his room might be searched at any moment. By early evening he was able to give a pretense of going out on a commission, and so escaped the hotel. With the jewel in his pocket he wandered the busy streets wondering anxiously what to do, and imagining in every man he passed a plain-clothes detective ready to apprehend him. Finally he decided to visit your aunt on Brixton-road. She had married a man named Oakshott, who used to fatten geese for the market. She was surprised to see him and asked why he was so pale, whereupon he replied that the whole affair of the stolen jewel at the hotel had upset him. He then went to the backyard and smoked a pipe over the problem. He remembered a friend in Kilburn, Maudsley, who had gone to the bad, and decided to take this man into his confidence. But as he recalled the agonies of his journey from the hotel, he wondered how he would carry the jewel safely to his friend; for at any moment he might be seized and searched, and the stone be found in his waistcoat pocket. As he continued to think on this dilemma his eyes fell upon a few geese that had waddled over and meandered about his feet. Suddenly an idea occurred to him. His sister had promised him a goose for Christmas, and he knew she would be as good as her word. He found a goose whose markings appeared unique—it had a barred tail of two dark bands—and he thrust the stone down the bird's gullet. The goose gave a cry and freed itself from his grasp, squawking and flying back into the flock just as your aunt poked her head out the back door.

" 'I've already felt for the fattest goose for you, Jem,' she cried. 'We fattened it even more expressly for you. It's there on the sideboard. We call it Jem's bird.'

" 'I'd rather have this one,' he said, running over and finding the goose with the double-barred tail and holding it up.

" 'The one inside is a good three pound heavier.'

" 'Thank you sister, but I much prefer this one.'

" 'Well, if you must,' she replied, a bit huffed. 'Kill it and take it with you.'

"Your father did as she bid and then carried the goose away to his friend. They shared a laugh over the whole business of the goose, but when your father finally opened up the bird he was amazed to find the stone missing! He hurried back to his sister who told him that *two* geese had had the markings he described, but that all the geese were gone—sold to market later that evening. Panicked, he ran to the market in search for the goose, but failed to get any information from the tight-lipped merchant who had bought the geese. I was following my own line of investigation which led to the same merchant when Dr. Watson and I chanced to come upon your father at that very moment, and I told him I knew the whereabouts of his goose. Delighted, he returned with us to our apartment, but once there I confronted him with his crime. He confessed everything to me. It was at that moment of the Christmas season, Miss Ryder, when I changed your family's life forever. I decided not to send your father to jail. I simply didn't think he needed it. Oh, I have let some persons out of my grasp before. But usually it was those who took private revenge against criminals who otherwise would have escaped through some technicality of the law. Only twice before have I let someone as plainly guilty as your father escape punishment. I am sorry to admit that in both those cases my judgment was later proved faulty. One was hung for a subsequent murder, while the other was later proved criminally insane. Now, on this Monday past, as though it were not enough for me to occasionally mull over these mistakes in judgment, I learned that you were abandoned over twelve years ago by the very man I had let go, a father who fancied that he ought to paint watercolours on the beaches of Ceylon rather than raise his own daughter! Three mistakes—three threads— Snap! Snap! Snap! I indeed wonder why I bestowed grace on any of them."

"Perhaps you are right, Mr. Holmes. Perhaps my father and these others should have been put in prison to learn their lessons. Yet the threat of punishment does not always stop men from their crimes."

"I did not say these other two were men."

Our visitor started. "Ah—"

"Exactly so, Miss Ryder. I meet with the unseemly in my line of work. You will excuse me if I do not always hold a chivalrous view. I have found that assumptions of innocence based on gender are not helpful to me."

"I suppose that's fair, Mr. Holmes," said she, and then with a relieved sigh, "In any event, your generosity to *me* has certainly been fair. The six pounds fifty will, in fact, help me a great deal."

"I did not say the draft was for six pounds fifty."

"Oh, I'm sorry—I thought that was the amount you said."

"The *violin* is worth six pounds fifty, yes. But I said I would compensate you for the *instrument* which, of course, includes the bow. And the bow is a Guarneri, one of the few that have survived from the early eighteenth century. The total of the violin and bow are on to three figures. The draft is for one-o-four."

"Oh, Mr. Holmes!"

"Well, I did say it would help pay for your education."

Miss Ryder objected at length, but finally gave up when she saw that Holmes would not make any concession in the matter. "My decision brought disaster to your family," he said, "and I consider this a minimal gesture."

"I shall never regard it so, Mr. Holmes."

"But the reason for your visit here still remains a mystery to Dr. Watson and me. Tell me, now, Miss Ryder, why you have come."

Chapter Two

The young lady locked her fingers into her upper palms and pressed her hands against each other in nervous agitation, finally unclasping them to take another sip from the teacup. Then she laid the saucer down and looked up with a worried expression.

"I came, Mr. Holmes, after reading that you sometimes keep your old apartments in London."

"Yes, usually in winter, when my bees in the country are dormant."

"It was reading about your bees that has led to my coming here today. I saw your article in the *Times:* 'Controlled Bee Stings Can Help Rheumatism.' "

"Yes. When applied directly to the afflicted area I have noticed occasional results."

"I was very encouraged from your article, Mr. Holmes, and cut it from the newspaper."

"Not for yourself, I suppose. To share it with whom? Your mother?"

"No, my father, Mr. Holmes. I had read a large retrospective on my father's work in *d'Object Art*. The article stated that he suffered from acute rheumatism, and had therefore given up painting and returned to the Continent. It even gave his two addresses. Until that moment I had no exact idea where my father had been living all these years. I had heard he was near India—but that was all. Now suddenly I learned he was in England, dividing his time between London and a villa in the country. I had often wondered as a child whether or not I would contact my father if I had the opportunity, and now I had that very decision before me. At first I vacillated. On the one hand I thought I would not go because of the hardships he had caused our family. Yet, perhaps now he was different, even changed. And unless I visited him, how would I know? I decided to send him your monograph about rheumatism, and see if he would respond. To my delight, he wrote back immediately."

"Do you have his letter with you?"

"Yes, here it is."

Holmes held it to the light. "Not much here—common stationary typed in single space with a signature at the bottom. Please go on, Miss Ryder."

"My father apologized for not writing earlier, but thought I would want nothing to do with him. He also said that a severe ailment of the legs and stomach kept him mostly confined to bed. He wished to see me, but preferred to wait a few weeks to see if he felt better. I replied by telling him of my upcoming studies at the British Museum in the fall, and of my summer plans to visit the professor's family with whom I would be staying. This time he telegrammed his reply. His health had grown even worse, but he still wanted to meet me. I suggested we meet at the West entrance to the British Museum at noon on the eighth of this month."

"That was yesterday. Did you tell your mother you would be meeting your father?"

"Oh, no. She would never approve. 'He is a black devil,' she always says, whenever the subject of my father comes up.

"And now I get to the queer part of my story, Mr. Holmes. I waited for my father at the West Entrance for three hours yesterday, but he never came. Of course, I was quite upset. Finally, I decided to take a cab to the London address shown on his envelope. I had ascended the steps and was about to ring the bell when an older-looking man in a beard opened the door as though to leave."

" 'Who are you?' he asked. He was startled, and it was clear he was not expecting anyone at the door. 'What do you want?' he demanded.

" 'Excuse me, sir,' I said, 'but I am looking for my father, Mr. James Ryder.'

"He looked quite puzzled. 'I live here, but have never heard of him,' he replied.

"I showed him one of my letters addressed to my father with the very street number at which we now stood. I then explained briefly why I was trying to meet him.

" 'I am quite amazed,' he replied, 'but I fear I cannot help you. Perhaps your father played a joke on you and wrote a wrong address on his letters.'

" 'But he responded to my letters from this address,' I cried, showing him an envelope from my father's correspondence. 'How could he have done so if he had not received them here?'

" 'I am very sorry, Mademoiselle, but I do not know your father and cannot help you. *Pardonnez-moi.*' He then disappeared behind the door, and I heard him throw the latch. I was left standing on the pavement without any idea of what next to do."

Again Holmes leaned forward and rubbed his hands together.

"You were only a young girl, Miss Ryder, when you last saw your father twelve years ago. Are you certain this man was not him?"

"This man was certainly not my father, Mr. Holmes."

"This fellow, then—can you describe him further?"

"Yes. He was clean-shaven—about sixty years old, I would say. Very aristocratic looking. French. Rather off-putting in his tone. Thin in the face, but with a heavy dark brow and beard, and with a bald spot in the midst of his graying hair."

"That is an excellent description."

"I have a picture of him, Mr. Holmes."

"Indeed! How did you manage that?"

"I drew a sketch of him late this afternoon. I thought it might help in finding my father."

"A very wise thing to have done," remarked Holmes, quite impressed. "I see the *Times* has not exaggerated your talent for portraiture. You clearly show this man's expression of contempt, yet apprehension. Do you yourself have any theory as to who this man is?"

"None at all, Mr. Holmes."

My companion joined the fingertips of his hands and sunk them into the ridge of his brow. Then he rose and stood before the fireplace with his chin against his breast and his hands thrust into his pockets. "Is there anything else that happened to you at the museum, Miss Ryder? Anything unusual?"

The lady thought for a moment. "Not at the British Museum, at least."

"Another place, then?"

"Well, there was one instance. I don't attach much importance to it. I visited the Louvre one day last spring. It was my first visit to Paris. As you probably know, the Louvre is a very long building—over half a mile long if you count the wings. There are many rooms and passageways that run adjacent to some of the gallery rooms, and I found myself briefly lost within one of these labyrinths. I kept to the halls but observed the rooms as I passed, for their doors were open. I am familiar with the materials of art and noticed many supplies inside the rooms: wooden panels, canvases, paints and brushes, smocks, and conservation and photographic equipment. I know that artists at the Louvre use such materials to make copies of famous paintings. A student paints a copy, and then an instructor points out the student's faults in colour gradation, perspective, light, and many other nuances that separate the student's work from a Master's. I stopped instantly at one room, however, when I saw two easels inside, and on one of them was the *Mona Lisa!* I was immediately drawn to it and walked into the room. Though no one was there I heard voices beyond an interior door that apparently led to another room. It was impossible not to hear bits and pieces of the conversation on the other side of the door. It sounded like a disagreement between two or three gentlemen, and I distinctly heard the words, '*Mona Lisa*' several times. I even thought I once heard my father's name, but no doubt I was mistaken. My attention soon returned to what I *thought* was the *Mona Lisa*."

"What do you mean by that, Miss Ryder?"

"There was a drape over just a corner of the painting. I was curious and lifted it up. To my surprise the portion underneath was unfinished. I then realized that this was only a copy of the *Mona Lisa*. The second easel was fully draped, but seeing that the painting on the first easel had been so wonderfully painted I lifted the sheet completely off it. To my amazement I now stood before the true *Mona Lisa*! I recognized the picture and its gilded frame from a postcard I own showing the *Mona Lisa* wall at the Salon Carré. Yet I looked back at the panel on the first easel. This painting, too, was no work of a student. The copy was, in fact, perfect in every other detail. Had it not been for the unfinished corner of the painting, the crazing of the original, and that the copy was unframed, I could not have known which was the real da Vinci. With my eyes I glanced back and forth rapidly from one painting to the other—an artist's trick that reveals differences. Yet the paintings remained indistinguishable to my eye. Even the smudges and marks on the right hand of the original were duplicated exactly, as were the abrasions around the mouth. At that moment I sensed someone's form and looked up. To my relief, it was only my own reflection in a full-length model's mirror that stood a short distance behind the pictures. I could see, however, the reflection of the backsides of the two paintings before me. Both works had been done on poplar wood—the green tint and grain of this wood are unmistakable. I wondered why a copyist should carry the imitation to such a degree. But then I recalled that wooden panels differ in colour and texture because of their plant species, and some artist's feel that these differences affect the tone of a painting, especially when the ground coat is thin. This copy, then, was the work of a modern perfectionist, though for what purpose I could not imagine. On the other hand, I admit to thinking it would make a marvelous forgery. Just then I heard voices growing louder and steps approaching the other side of the interior door. I hastened to lower the cloth over the *Mona Lisa* and had just retreated into the hall when I heard the doorknob turn and someone enter the room. I was afraid, and waited for a voice to hail me. But apparently I had escaped unnoticed. I still thought about returning to the room to pretend I was seeing the interior for the first time—I wanted so much to meet whatever hand it was that painted so wonderfully. But my fear proved greater than my curiosity, and except for noting the room number above the door as C-two-two-one-two I continued down the passageway as noiselessly as possible. In a moment I was relieved to find myself back among the galleries."

"Why did you note the room number? asked Holmes."

"I thought during a less delicate moment I might return some day to meet the artist."

"And your father—Did he ever say he frequented the Louvre?"

"Not that I recall."

"Did he reference anyone in his letters—friends, artists, professionals of any kind?"

"No, Mr. Holmes. Well, except for my mother. He asked about her welfare."

"Nothing else?"

"No."

"And did your mother respond?"

"Not that I know of."

Holmes was silent for a moment. As he had grown older he often pondered a matter for some time before he put a 'yea' or 'nay' to his willingness to investigate a case. "I will look into this problem about your father, Miss Ryder," he finally said.

The look of anxiety clouding our visitor's face fell in an instant. "Then I am much relieved, Mr. Holmes. I can hardly thank you enough."

"A trip to Paris, however, may be necessary," said Holmes as he drew out a piece of paper from a nearby table drawer. "I believe you said the number of the room where you saw the *Mona Lisa* was C-two-one-two-two."

"No, Mr. Holmes. I said, 'C-two-two-*one*-two'."

"Ah, so you did. You're sure of that, then?"

"Yes. The first two numbers were my exact age at the time, and the last two would have been my poor brother's. I made this association to help me remember it."

"You had a brother? He is no longer living?"

"No, he died of scarlet fever as a child."

"How old was he?"

"In a month he would have been four. He died in December on my mother's birthday, a few days, in fact, from my own. Every year now finds our spirits in the same terrible state. What for others is a season of merriment is only a time of gloom and sadness for us."

"I understand," said Holmes with more empathy than I might have expected. "Well, the matter grows even more obscure, Miss Ryder."

"It does?"

"Yes, but it might be helpful if you could come to 721 Montague Street at 10:00 tomorrow morning. It is next to the British Museum. Can you meet us there?"

"Certainly, Mr. Holmes."

"Till tomorrow, then."

With a delicate grace characteristic of her whole manner, Rachel Ryder carefully adjusted her thin wrap, hat, and coat, and departed to a waiting carriage below.

"A most curious case, Watson," said Holmes, as he took his pipe and filled it with some tobacco from his coat pocket.

"What do you make of it all, Holmes?"

"Trouble, Watson! Trouble for our young friend, and trouble for her father, if he is alive. Take Miss Ryder's discovery of a copy of the *Mona Lisa*, for example. I would not normally attach any importance to it, and yet because of the painting's theft—" Holmes stopped in mid-sentence to wave his pipe in a silent gesture of protest.

"You suspect there is some connection between the copy and her missing father?" I asked.

"I find it remarkable, at least, that the portrait she drew exactly resembles the Director of the Louvre, Mssr. Bantok. I also note with interest the identity of the room number at he Louvre. I have, in fact, made written inquiries to this very address on certain occasions in recent years. It is the office of Peter Vernet, my cousin."

"Not your French relative, Holmes?"

"The same."

"He has an English name, then?"

"He was named for our grandfather."

"Is he the one I met outside your old lodgings at Montague Street alongside the British Museum?"

"No, that was his older brother, Robert, who assumed my lease and made it possible for me to take these apartments here at Baker Street. Robert was a fellow at the Museum."

"Both of these brothers are artists, then?"

"Yes, but Peter is the more gifted one. He shares an office rented by the Louvre at the British Museum and shares his time between there and Paris. His knowledge of stolen Renaissance art is second to none in Europe. His own paintings are even more remarkable than his specialized knowledge of forgery. I doubt if there is anyone as good as he is in the rendering of an object or a style. He would have been famous in any other generation. Unfortunately, he finds his works of realism ignored by collectors who never tire of Impressionism, a movement he regards as a bad joke."

"Well, I would disagree with him there."

"I fear your taste is bourgeois, Watson, and is very typical of the attitude that drives this demand for inferior art."

"Everyone else seems to like Impressionism, Holmes. The works are so dream-like and colourful. And they remain fresh with the public even after decades!"

"Still," said Holmes, as he snuggled into his armchair with the air of a man who was about to relish delivering a short lecture upon an indulging friend, "both Peter and I would consider such emotions misdirected. Be careful that you yourself don't follow the Impressionists into a mindless definition of art. Their followers can be a vicious sort, too. Vernet's brother, Robert, caused a furor with his statement in *d'Object Art,* when he said that their self-congratulatory and sensual remarks often gush forth like soiled shirt cuffs from within fine coat sleeves. Shortly afterward he was beaten nearly senseless as he returned home from a university art forum where he had again spoken vehemently against them. Impressionism, *indeed!* Yes, there is falsehood there, Watson!"

I truly pitied Robert Vernet, but was nevertheless dismayed at Holmes's strong feelings on the subject of Impressionism. "I'm very sorry about your cousin, Holmes," said I, "but still, I don't see what any of this has to do with Miss Ryder's case."

"No? I'm surprised, Watson. Within all the best museums are strong loyalties for one epoch of art over another. Last year's theft at the Louvre has merely heightened this tension. For example, we know that *the* da Vinci masterpiece was stolen eight months ago, and that prior to its theft Rachel

Ryder overheard an argument about this very painting. Her chance encounter may mean nothing. On the other hand, it may mean a great deal. Are the existing rivalries getting out of hand at the Louvre? Did someone within the museum cause its disappearance? It seems to me that one's view of art has much to do with the case, especially if you are a board member of the Louvre about to disperse large sums of money on *this* style versus *that*.

"I thought the Louvre's purpose was to simply house great art. I didn't think they were subject to society's whim and fancy."

"That used to be the case, Watson, but the Louvre is a public institution, and public mood has changed. No longer do people agree upon what is great art. Nowadays there is considerable restlessness among the public and a demand for musty institutions like the Louvre to justify its choices and to explain its relevance. The personnel at most large museums practically line up with bayonets against each other when the cause is something akin to Ryder versus the Renaissance."

"I thought that recent paintings went to the Musée d' Orsay."

Some do, yes. But the d' Orsay has its disciples at the Louvre, too. They are always pushing for changes."

"And you are among those who prefer the older art?"

"I contend, at least, that art must be truthful, Watson. The definition of fine art must conform to logic. The best art is defined by the philosopher who says, 'There is only one thing certain,' to which his fellow queries, 'What is that?,' to which the philosopher rejoins, '*Just that.*' "

"I don't understand, Holmes."

"It's a kind of philosopher's merry-go-round, Watson. The one thing certain is that one thing is certain. I'm saying in a round about way—sorry for the pun—that the finest art is always self evidently so. When people call inferior art the best art, it is because they no longer accept its obvious qualities. They are merely reacting with emotion."

"I still don't fully see how all this relates to the case at hand."

"Permit me a brief example about Impressionism, then, Watson, if only that it might ultimately bear on Miss Ryder's problem."

"By all means, Holmes."

"You would probably agree with those who say that the Impressionists' eye is more truthful about observation than any other."

"I've heard that said about them."

"The Impressionist sees a boat far out on the water, but does not paint the porthole bolts into his canvas because he cannot see them. He is right about this, and argues that the classicist, i.e., the type of painter who puts every possible detail into a painting, is wrong to put the porthole bolts into his picture merely because he *knows* they are there. The Impressionist understands that the classicist is not being truthful about observation. So far, so good. But then I find the same Impressionist likely to omit the porthole bolts if the boat is docked and standing two feet away from him! Impressionist paintings are full of this arbitrary approach; it makes even their close-up portraits blurry. These same observations about Impressionism were what landed Robert in so much trouble after the forum he attended."

"I don't think Impressionists are trying to be literalists, Holmes. They're just reacting subjectively to what is around them."

"Exactly! Thank you, Watson. That is why neither Impressionism nor Classicism gives the world the best art. The Romantic Impressionist asks us to put aside our brains to embrace whatever his vision chooses, while the Classicist insists on the 'omniscience' to see things that aren't there."

"But what art is left, Holmes, if you reject these two approaches?"

"*Just that*," he replied, pointing to a bi-folded calling card on the fireplace mantle a few feet above his head. Holmes sat up and with two fingers and in one motion plucked the card from its perch and spun it into my lap from across the room.

"Mssr. Bantock, Director, Louvre, Paris." said I, reading the card. "Paul Vernet's room number is hand written beneath it. I don't understand, Holmes."

"No, no. Turn the card over."

I did as Holmes bid and saw a photographic vignette of the *Mona Lisa*.

"*That*, Watson," added Holmes reverently, "is true art."

"So you believe that Renaissance art is the best art?"

"Not all Renaissance art, Watson, but certainly da Vinci's *Mona Lisa* qualifies."

"This defining of art seems a bit cerebral, Holmes."

"Not the mind, Watson—the eye! Great painting requires *observation*. And what other painting better demonstrates the painter's eye than the *Mona Lisa?* The Lady herself is focused wonderfully to the eye, because she is the subject. The landscape behind her is less important and remains less focused accordingly. Da Vinci, you see, was a master observer. He was a master craftsman, too, and as Ruskin says; 'When craftsmanship is combined with the heart, a work of art results.' This is why the *Mona Lisa* has been the centerpiece of the world's best-known museum. Need we question why someone should have stolen it?"

"For money, I should think."

"For money only? Then why hasn't the thief returned it by some intermediate means and collected the rewards being offered? No, I think the thief is a cultivated soul—twisted in his morality no doubt, but one who wants an object of perfection."

"Thief, and not thieves, Holmes? There is only one?"

"It is the individual who is most often affected by megalomania, Watson. It takes many factors for a group of people to become equally obsessed, whereas a moment's unchecked passion in the individual can lead him quickly toward some rash act that is mindless of its consequences. I think when the *Mona Lisa* is finally found the criminal will turn out to be some impetuous fellow. But I'll never fault his taste in art! The question before us, then, Watson, is whether this person is connected to the disappearance of James Ryder. Thankfully, we already have in Miss Ryder's sketch a definite clue. The old bearded man who opened the door and talked to her on that London street was certainly the Director of the Louvre, Mssr. Bantok."

"You have met him, then?"

"Twice. It is not surprising he is in London. According to the *Pall Mall,* the Louvre is considering James Ryder's work for purchase. It would be natural for the Director to make an initial inquiry here in London before bringing Ryder's work before the Board."

"Your explanation sounds logical."

"Probability lies in that direction. What else do we know about James Ryder?"

"I read an extended piece on him in today's *Times.* Here it is, Holmes."

"Excellent, Watson. Yes, the Louvre is considering a purchase of his works—that we know. Ah, here is something else; Ryder's first paintings of Ceylon were of native houses decorated in peculiar Christmas attire—dead monkeys hung from the lintels."

"How horrible, Holmes!"

"Their Christmas goose, I suppose. Does this suggest anything to you?"

"Nothing at all."

"In this instance it is the common fact we are after. It lays hidden behind that grotesque image of the simian that would divert us. To wit, if Ryder arrived in Ceylon at the beginning of winter, then he would have departed from England four or five months earlier in the middle of autumn."

"Why is that important?"

"It means he left England knowing another child would be born to him."

"How do you deduce that?"

"Miss Ryder mentioned that her brother's birthday was celebrated a month later than her mother's. Her mother's birthday was in December, so the son's was in January. According to Miss Ryder the son would now be twelve years old had he lived. We know from our own case notes that we met Ryder in late December 1898, and this article tells us that Ryder left for Ceylon in autumn of 1899. You might remember that Ryder promised he would flee the country so the case would break down against Horner the plumber. It became unnecessary, of course, because we recovered the jewel, and gave that stone, along with certain other evidence, to the police. But to Ryder the idea of living abroad was probably planted in his mind at that time."

"What is the significance of all this?"

"Do the math, Watson. The mother would have been with child for about six months at the time her husband deserted her, so certainly he knew about his wife's condition."

"Ah!—the scoundrel!"

"Yes, precisely. But what does it all mean?"

"You must have some speculation about it, Holmes."

My friend shrugged his shoulders with an air of indifference. "They would only be guesses, Watson," he said quietly.

"But if you *were* to guess, Holmes?"

Sherlock Holmes laughed. "Well, Watson, it's true there is nothing else to engage our attention this evening; if you really must know, I would say a number of possibilities exist. For example, was Ryder's weak nature overwhelmed by the knowledge of having to care for another child? We know his own sense of inadequacy from our encounter with him years ago. That is one possibility. On the other hand, are the newspapers merely editorializing when they conjure up the pining woman role, admirably filled in this case by Mrs. Ryder, who was convenient enough to be a handsome woman in distress and whose condition practically invited the attentions of gentlemen—to wit, what if the child were not Ryder's own? That would put things on a much different footing, would it not? Ryder's departure may have been the sudden and disillusioned choice of a devastated husband."

"It appears to me that he deserted his daughter in any case."

"Quite so, Watson. And yet let us consider Miss Ryder's case from a different angle altogether. Are we to believe her when she tells us that her father is trying to mend his relationship with her?"

"You suspect her of lying? I thought she was entirely genuine—perfectly charming."

"She might be telling us what she *thinks* are the facts about her father, but does that mean she is correct? For example, can we be sure James Ryder is even alive?"

"Not living? I don't understand, Holmes."

"Let me rephrase—how do we know that James Ryder is really the author of Miss Ryder's letter and telegram, or that he has returned to England?"

"I thought those facts were well established."

"Are they? No one from London seems to have known Ryder before his years in Ceylon. His wife does not communicate with him. His daughter has not met him since his return. He excuses his first meeting with her by claiming to be ill, and fails to appear during a second appointment. He communicates by typewriter and telegram instead of handwritten letters which would clearly identify him. All we have is one signature and the only photograph of him in any of the newspapers is this small, blurry one in the *Times*. So how can we be sure this man who corresponds with Rachel Ryder is her father?"

"I see what you mean, Holmes. You're implying that perhaps Ryder never returned from Ceylon—that someone, a thief perhaps, might have stolen Ryder's paintings—perhaps even have killed him—and is now impersonating him."

"It would explain the facts, Watson, at least as we know them. Of course, this is only one possibility, and I confess to a bias on the point that such a scenario would be in keeping with my current theory that such human beings as James Ryder are unlikely to change their moral compass in any real way. So I am not convinced that Ryder cares for his daughter—for I don't know if he is even alive."

"If that is the case, Holmes, you would do harm by revealing the truth to Miss Ryder. She would be devastated to discover that her father is dead, for she thinks he is living and vitally interested in her welfare."

"I'm aware of that, Watson. A visit to-morrow to the apartment address of James Ryder might be helpful. We will go there after we see my cousin, Vernet. I think a little sleep is in order now, my dear fellow, for tomorrow promises to be a busy day."

Chapter Three

The next morning found Rachel Ryder already standing on the pavement at the address on Montague Street when we arrived. I still read worry in her features, but Holmes assured her that she had reason to hope, and his confident manner had its usual effect of putting his client at ease. Holmes had sent a telegram to Vernet earlier in the morning to alert him of our arrival, but when the landlady showed us up to Vernet's room we were disappointed to find he was not there. We decided to wait, and I took this opportunity to look at the space where Holmes had begun his detective career. By any standards it was a modest and featureless apartment. The single room was windowless and small, and there was a bed in one corner. Its sparse furnishings and peeling wallpaper added to its depressing atmosphere. A group of dilapidated arrow-back chairs surrounded a small, leafless, brown table in the middle of the room. Besides these deficiencies, the apartment was also wanting in fresh air, and I wondered how long we would be keeping our vigil. We had not waited more than five minutes, however, when the outside door banged, and we heard a shouted announcement from the landlady followed by a frenzied footfall upon the stair. A young man of about thirty appeared in the doorway, pale and worn. His face was haggard, his cheeks gaunt and colourless, his eyes afire with sleeplessness or drink. His thin shoulders heaved and sagged, and his whole manner of dress and toilet showed a harried and exhausted state.

"Holmes, you must help me!" he sputtered, in a French accent.

"Vernet! Watson, if you will!" exclaimed Holmes, beckoning for help. I urged upon Vernet his own chair and a tonic, both of which he accepted with a grateful nod, and while his composure returned he kept nodding sporadically as though affirming to all present that what he had to say would justify our hearing it.

"I don't think I have seen you, Vernet, since that small incident over the Raphael," said my friend.

"This is worse, Holmes. Much worse!" said he, throwing up his hands. "Something has gone terribly wrong! This lady's father was arrested in London yesterday afternoon!"

"James Ryder?"

"Yes."

"And you know this lady?"

"I know of her," said he, with an admiring glance toward our fair young companion.

"So James Ryder has been arrested again," exclaimed Holmes with disgust, and adding under his breath "if so it be he!" "Well, then," said Holmes in his normal voice again, "nothing changes in thirteen years. For what was he arrested?"

"For the crime of stealing Botticelli's *Little Sisters* from the Louvre."

"Thievery again! I wonder why I thought he might have changed. Pshaw! It's all the old story again! But you have our full attention, Vernet."

Holmes' cousin was obviously shaken by his circumstances, and I noticed small tremors of his fingers occasionally echo through his limbs in tiny spasmodic jerks. Clearly he was too overcome with emotion to give a clear and logical presentation to his story, and when he finally spoke it came in halting spurts amidst agonized utterances and sporadic blank moments of silence. For the benefit of my readers I have smoothed out the rough valleys of this young man's remarkable narrative.

"Thank you for this," said Vernet, as he took a long drink from the glass I handed him. "I begin to feel better. I won't keep you gentlemen waiting, nor you, Mademoiselle. I have been to your apartment, Holmes, and back again within the last half-hour. I feel quite the fool already. I hope Miss Ryder will excuse what I say about her father. But the urgency of the moment demands a bald account of the facts that will not stand much delicacy."

"Of course," she replied.

I could tell, however, that the apprehension of hearing more unfortunate news about her father was beginning to tell upon Rachel Ryder's countenance.

"And you, Holmes, will have to wade through my incoherence," remarked Vernet. "But here are the facts. The police have accused Ryder of stealing the Botticelli, and indeed, they found it in his room at the Commonds."

"I thought he stayed at an apartment, said Holmes."

"He briefly took a room at the Commonds during a showing of his paintings in the hotel's lobby."

"I see."

"But the Director will not allow me to examine the Botticelli to authenticate it, and I am sure it is a copy."

"It was just hanging on the wall, then, and the police walked in?"

"No, it was found in a closet. An anonymous tip was given to the police."

"And how can you be certain it is a forgery since you have not examined it?"

Vernet hesitated. "I would rather not answer that."

"Is it not because you yourself made the forgery?"

Vernet sprang from his chair in agitation and clapped his hands in despair. "How do *you* know about my copy, Holmes?"

"You do not deny making it, then?"

"I deny making a forgery. I made a copy only."

"And what is the difference?"

The visage of Holmes's cousin slowly changed, and his body deflated back into the chair. "A very big difference," he said quietly, gazing away. "A very big difference, and yet—no difference at all."

"*Now*—," said Holmes, briefly holding out his folded hands with his index fingers pointing to his relative, "—*now* you may begin at the beginning."

"Yes, Holmes. And you will see that I am not at fault as you suspect. A little, perhaps, but only a little."

"We are all listening."

Peter Vernet took a deep breath as though he saw himself before a great precipice.

"It all began about a year ago, Holmes, several months before the *Mona Lisa* was stolen from the Museum. I was copying a small Botticelli piece using the flat Giotto technique of thinned egg tempera, when the Director, Mssr. Bantock, entered my room from his private office. He had rarely shown any interest in my painting, but now he began praising it at length and marveling at the exactness of my copy.

" 'Brilliant work, Vernet!' he cried. 'Your work equals your reputation.'

" 'My reputation? I don't believe I have—'

" 'Nonsense! I have talked with a few of your patrons. They were most impressed by the commissions you carried out for them. In fact, they all said they were planning new commissions for you.'

" 'They did?'

" 'But a greater proposal than these is at hand. I hardly exaggerate in saying it will be the most important work of your life. Someone is in my office this very moment to explain it to you. Follow me.'

"I did as he bid, and retired to the Director's office. As I entered I saw a man across the room, a tall, aristocratic-looking English gentleman of about thirty-five, with his chin raised in contemplation of a red chalk drawing of a young man by the Italian artist, del Sarto. Hearing us enter he turned his head to face us, removed a cigar from his mouth, and without turning his body surveyed each one of us in turn with his narrow eyes. 'I much prefer the *machismo* of the Spanish to the Italian,' said he, pointing to the chalk drawing above his head. 'I have just come from Brentano's gallery where I was considering a Velasquez. I only wish its documentation was more satisfying.'

" 'Perhaps we can help you,' replied the Director. 'My associate here, Peter Vernet, tells me a chemical test can now be done to show whether a certain green paint used by Velasquez is really from the seventeenth century.'

" 'Really? How is that possible?'

" 'A hypodermic syringe is poked through the canvas to collect the paint which is then tested by a chemical analysis.'

" 'But alas—I have no syringe.'

" 'I have one here,' replied the Director, taking a key from his pocket and unlocking a side drawer to pull out a needle and its case. He opened the box and set it before the man who then gazed at the hypodermic syringe for a long moment until a bead of sweat appeared on his forehead.

" 'I doubt that the owner would trust me to take the Velasquez from his Gallery," said the man, "but perhaps if I could borrow this instrument for the day, Monsieur? I promise to return it in the morning.'

" 'Fine!' said the Director. 'Put the sample in this small capsule. We will test it right here at the Museum. There will be no charge, of course. Please—' said he, motioning each of us to some chairs that surrounded an oblong mahogany table in the midst of a room lined with glass casings filled with art objects.

" 'This visitor, Peter,' said the Director, addressing me with a pained expression on this face, 'is Wolfgang Kern. He is here to make an offer. Mr. Kern claims he can restore the *Mona Lisa* to the Louvre. He asks in exchange that the Louvre grant him the Dictatorship—er—the Directorship to the Museum within two years. Of course, the Directorship has never gone to anyone but a Frenchman, and naturally it would be a great personal sacrifice for any connoisseur, such as myself, to offer the helm of the Museum to a mere figurehead. Nevertheless, I am prepared to make this sacrifice if it will benefit the Museum and the French people.' This short speech seemed to exhaust the Director, and he lapsed into silence as he mopped his forehead and hunched over the table, no doubt despairing about his future.

" 'Tut, tut, Mssr. Bantock,' replied Kern, 'You look as though the world has been unkind to you. You should be happy to play a part in the *Mona Lisa's* recovery.'

" 'The pleasure of helping you is all mine,' replied Bantock with complete emptiness of feeling.

" 'Now, then, Mssr. Vernet,' said Kern, turning to me, 'I will tell you my plan, and the Director will have the advantage of hearing it again. It is quite ingenious, is it not, Mssr. Director?'

" 'Oui, oui, most ingenious.'

" 'Here it is, then. You, Vernet, will complete your copy of the *Mona Lisa* to the best of your amazing ability. We will place the copy at the villa of James Ryder, a client of mine. Then we will give the police an anonymous tip that the da Vinci is there."

"I have heard of this man, Ryder."

"His notoriety is growing, and I represent his art to collectors and institutions. James Ryder has agreed to participate in this plan to recover the *Mona Lisa*. He and I will be crossing the

Atlantic during the time the police investigate his house. We will be on our way to America to promote his art."

" 'How will you restore this man's reputation?' I asked.

" 'We won't—not for a week, at least, or perhaps even for a month. No, wait! Listen to my plan before passing judgment, Vernet! The initial hullabaloo over 'recovering' the *Mona Lisa* will be done primarily by the police and the newspapers. The Louvre will also spread plenty of bogus rumors that week confirming that your painting is the true da Vinci. But the museum will avoid making an official pronouncement over it, claiming that to do so is the domain and right of the Director who is vacationing somewhere in the mountains and cannot be reached. During the first few days immediately following the police's 'recovery', I will arrange for at least one newspaper to remind the public that Dr. Watson, the biographer of the detective Sherlock Holmes, published a story some years ago actually claiming that Ryder once stole a valuable jewel. So the public will be quite convinced that Ryder is the obvious suspect in the theft of the *Mona Lisa*. All during that week Ryder will be vilified in the newspapers. Immediately afterward he will be exonerated when the Director announces that the real *Mona Lisa* has just been found in the Museum, and that what had been found at Ryder's house a week ago must therefore have been a copy. But the resulting *cause celébrè*, so dear to every artist's heart, will by then have already surrounded Ryder in a melee. This memorable public reaction will be our atonement to him for having endured all this. The scandal will indeed help him in his American tour this fall. Yes! Yes!' cried Kern, his eyes gleaming, 'it will generate a lot of curiosity among the public. I hope, in fact, it will catapult his work into having a place in next year's New York Armory Show alongside Picasso, Braque and Duchamp. It will be a lovely scandal with great results, and I will offer the Louvre first options on any, *or all*, of Ryder's work.'

"The Director kept his head bowed and shook it slowly back and forth with incredulous snorts.

" 'I want to understand this matter clearly, Monsieur,' I replied. 'Are you saying that I must make two copies? For you say that the police will find one painting at the villa, and that the Director will find another at the Louvre.'

" 'There are not two copies,' replied Kern, 'We do not ask you to invest more of your time or the Museum's expense to make another copy. There is another way. I have told my plan to the police inspector who will be in charge of the painting's 'recovery' at the villa, and he has agreed to give the Louvre your painting after the first week. He will do it under cover at night.'

'Won't that reflect poorly on him the next day when the newspapers think that the *Mona Lisa* has been stolen again?'

" 'I believe the newspapers will put two and two together and see that the painting disappeared the very night before another painting, also thought to be the *Mona Lisa,* was found at the Louvre. Journalists are bound to suggest that the Louvre arranged to have the police's copy returned to the Museum secretly in order to save the Louvre final embarrassment. For the Louvre will salvage some of its reputation if the public can be convinced that the *Mona Lisa* was never really stolen, but only displaced within the museum. The police inspector can even be touted as a coy and clever fellow for going behind closed doors with the Louvre in all of this.'

" 'But Ryder can still be accused of having once tried to steal the *Mona Lisa.*'

" 'No one will really care enough at that point to bring him to trial. Either the real *Mona Lisa* will have been recovered by then—'

" 'How is that possible?'

" 'I will explain that in a moment—again, either the real *Mona Lisa* will have been recovered by then, or what is *thought* by the public to be the *Mona Lisa* will have been

37

'recovered'. Either way James Ryder is willing to go into the history books as a thief twice unsuccessful if there is a chance that the true *Mona Lisa* can be recovered.'

" 'That would be quite a sacrifice.'

" 'What? Oh, yes, I suppose. Well, that is not my business, really. As to authenticating your copy, Vernet, the Louvre's photographs showing the highly detailed crazing of the *Mona Lisa* will be substituted with photographs of your own painting. The photographs will be a precaution in case some connoisseur bears immediate pressure on us to provide public authentication. The many *Mona Lisa* postcards, *et cetera,* owned by the public will be said by the Louvre to have come from a copy whose whereabouts are no longer known. But all will go well, especially when a parade of unsuspecting government officials and a number of newspapermen accompany your painting to the *Mona Lisa's* original position on the wall. Imagine it, Peter! Your work hanging in the most coveted two-foot-square space in the art world. What do you say to that?'

" 'I could not possibly agree to anything of the kind.'

" 'What! Why not? You think it dishonest, do you? Come, Vernet! This is hardly a time to quibble like a child!'

" 'It would be *more* than dishonest,' I replied. 'If accepted as the original, my imitation would be the embodiment of the Renaissance's highest ideals as understood by Leonardo. It is all false. Nor can I believe that Director Bantock would agree to your plan for a moment.'

"The Director had remained silent throughout Kern's exposition, his shoulders bent over the table in defeat. 'It is even worse than that, *mon ami*,' he said to me at last, holding his head limply in his hands. 'If the *Mona Lisa* is not recovered, the Louvre has agreed, for Leonardo's sake, to publicly admit after a month of the plan that your painting is not his. But even then I fear that Mssr. Kern can take advantage of the situation for his own ends. It will turn into an

opportunity for him, [...]
have argued before about [...]
  " 'No, Mssr. Director, [...]
not argue; we merely discu[ss ...]
  " 'I know how your min[d ...]
voice rising. 'You will seize [...]
base fellows at the newspapers. [...]
perception is the only consideratio[n ...]
the public preferred Vernet's imitatio[n ...] ..nci
original. 'Was not the same awe expre[ssed ...] ..nitation
as over the original? Was not the fee[ling of] pleasure the
same?' Thus will you argue that truth is irrelevant when
viewing art. And when I take issue with what you say, you
will tell the public even cleverer lies. I have heard your lofty
twaddle before. You will tell them the democratic spirit in
France must no longer tolerate the burdensome verdicts of past
generations—that too many art critics for centuries have
blindly forged their judgments in the furnaces of aristocratic
and monarchial cultures. Rather, if the French people believe
something to be so, let it is so! And if a false *Mona Lisa*
arouses the same passions within the bosom of the Frenchman,
then, *vive la difference!*'

  " 'A very colourful statement,' said Kern, amused. 'I only
wish I understood it. What you say about me is actually not
my view at all.' Then turning to me, he said, 'As to your
falsehood hanging on the wall, Peter, well—this state of affairs
will only last a short time. We only ask that you comply with
our plan for up to a month, if necessary. Thirty short days,
Vernet, that is all we ask!'

  " 'But exactly how will my copy help the painting be
found?'

  " 'A fair question,' he said boldly, then briefly muttering into
his chin, 'if not a formidable one! Let me explain it to you.
Let us pretend that you are the thief who stole the *Mona Lisa*.'

  " 'Me?'

...s pass after your theft and ... on everyone's lips—the da Vinci ...enly the money you dreamed of getting ...ollector means little more than soap bubbles to ...curator or expert will grant the authenticity of your ...ing, and without this endorsement your oil is only worth the price of a clever copy. You sell it immediately.'

" 'Why would I do that?'

" 'Public sentiment will be focused upon the *Mona Lisa*. The desire for a fine copy will be at its peak. Suspicion is no longer a factor.'

" 'But I *know* I have the original.'

" 'Do you? Within a day of the Director's 'discovery' of the *Mona Lisa*, he will further announce to the papers that a mistake occurred in the Museum. A copy of the *Mona Lisa* had accidentally been hung in the place of the real *Mona Lisa* some weeks before the theft. What had been stolen then, and eventually sold to Ryder, was only a copy. As it turns out, the real *Mona Lisa* was under a sheet on an easel in the room of one, P. Vernet. The Director will recall that months ago he had noticed Vernet painting a copy of the *Mona Lisa,* but never gave it much thought. Suspecting now that there might have been an accidental switch, the Director compared the photographic evidence in the archives with what he had thought was a mere copy, and behold, it was the *Mona Lisa*! Vernet, as it turns out, had indeed made an excellent copy of the *Mona Lisa* and then entrusted the return of the real *Mona Lisa* to one of his apprentices. The apprentice mistook the copy for the original, placed it into the *Mona Lisa's* frame, and so hung the copy on the wall. Even you, or rather the thief, I mean, will be fooled into thinking he only has a copy.'

" 'But when the real thief hears of this, he might become angry and destroy the original,' I cried.

" 'Nonsense, Vernet! Certainly he will be angry, but so what? It's still worth money! He's a thief, isn't he? Money, and more money—that's what a thief thinks about! Any other motivations such as a real aesthetic attraction to the painting must be secondary to him. No, a real admirer would have respected da Vinci too much to commit such villainy! The thief will have to settle for what money he can get. But we do not want to make him too angry, so Director Bantock has sweetened the honey pot for him. The Director has secretly contacted the owners of all the major galleries in France, Italy, England, and Germany, and offered them a goodly sum for any da Vinci replicas that come into their shops. In this way we hope to recover the da Vinci. So there is my plan, Mssr. Vernet. We already have the essential personnel from the Louvre agreeing to it. But of course it cannot take place without your consent. You are essential to the plan, for you will need to finish the copy. What do you say?'

"You can imagine, Holmes, that as I listened to Kern I had mixed feelings about such a plan. Before I could ever agree, I would need to know more about it.

" 'Please' I asked, 'explain again why the painting would first be 'found' at your client's house, then 'found' a week later at the Museum.'

"Is it not obvious?" replied Kern. "The Louvre's Director could not feign a positive identification in both cases, for that would totally discredit him. The reason why the painting must ultimately be 'found' at the Museum by the Louvre is to vindicate Ryder and prove him innocent. Otherwise Ryder would forever be thought guilty by the public.'

" 'Now I understand,' I replied.

Holmes leaned back in his chair and stroked the side of his chin with his hand. "This man Kern seems to be an interesting and formidable fellow," said my friend quietly.

"That's it exactly, Holmes. The Director and I are no match for him."

"And I presume if the da Vinci is not recovered you will be embarrassed to admit that you hung your copy in Leonardo's spot."

"Correct again, Holmes. Yet, as I discussed these matters with the Director and Kern I could not deny the feeling that the whole *raison d'etrê* of my artistic ability, if not my whole existence, was fated for this very hour—to help recover da Vinci's masterpiece and return it to its rightful place. As I wondered what to do I glanced at the Director, but gathered from his gloomy countenance that he believed doom would overtake us in any event. There was yet one factor to consider.

" 'Why James Ryder?' I asked. 'I've heard the name, but who exactly is he?'

"Kern narrowed contemptuous eyes toward me as though inspecting a worm. 'J. Leslie Ryder is the next star in the constellation of Master artists,' replied he with an offended tone. 'Do you see Orion chased from his hunting fields, or the Great Bear and her cubs hiding in a cave? Pisces swims away in despair, and Taurus returns to his stall like a humble milking kine. They all make room for the meteoric J. Leslie Ryder, who emblazons the sky with the light of his art.'

"The Director jerked his head back and laughed derisively at Kern's ridiculous speech. 'You're mad!' cried he. 'He paints mountains like triangles, and draws trees and houses like balls and squares. He paints no better than a child! And listen to you talk! You've picked up the patter of the American Medicine Man! Perhaps you have a magic tonic to grow hair on our heads, too—no? Hee, hee! 'Pisces swims away.' Hee, hee!' The Director patted a bald spot on his head.

" 'No, no, Mssr. Bantok,' countered Kern, pointing a reproving finger, 'there are not enough superlatives to describe Ryder's genius. All men like he are despised at the beginning. Yes, it is true I have made some money selling his art. What of it! I understand his art. And I will communicate it to the world.'

Sell it to the world is more like it,' replied the Director.

" 'I'm sure Mssr. Vernet sees through your jealously, Bantok. Your head is buried in the sands of the fifteenth century where you look in vain for your meaningless art relics which you love more than women! Bah! What is the use of making someone like you understand? No matter. In the future, men like me will raise the masses to a new understanding. We will tell them what to like and what to hate. For example, when I am the Director I will not immediately say, 'da Vinci is bad!' No, that would be foolish! We of the new school can use people's deeply held beliefs about da Vinci to our advantage. For if we said, 'da Vinci is bad, and Ryder is good,' no one would believe us at first. So we will say, 'da Vinci is good, and Ryder is good,' because this way Ryder is understood to be good in a way that people understand.'

" 'You are abominable,' cried the Director.

"Kern smiled. 'We will bombard them with whatever messages we wish, and give them no rest or quarter! It will be only a matter of time before we have them thinking that they are stupid if they do not agree with us. Even da Vinci will not remain sacred without our approval. Yes, the time will come when we will be able to say, 'da Vinci is bad!' '

" 'So you believe that da Vinci is a bad relic from the fifteenth century?' I cried. 'You *are* most untrue, sir. I will never participate in your scheme.'

" 'Peter, you are so stubborn,' said Kern, amused. 'Don't you care about the Museum and the *Mona Lisa's* recovery? I was only using da Vinci as a hypothetical example. I do not really believe he is bad! Da Vinci is good! But not for the reasons you think. Da Vinci was good because he was different. And therein lay his genius. He was a craftsman because he was unique, not because he could paint people and objects realistically. A true craftsman is simply an artist who brings his own vision to the world. It doesn't matter if paintings are scribble. It is originality that matters. That is why James Ryder is such an important artist. If only all painters saw as he.'

" 'So you only admire works of uniqueness?'

" 'Yes.'

" 'Yet you still want a copy of the *Mona Lisa?*'

" 'Well, yes.'

" 'Then you admit that your scheme requires me to paint in such a way as to bring nothing unique to the world. You are quite the hypocrite, Monsieur. On the one hand you insist that artists be original, yet on the other hand you beg me for a mere imitation.'

" 'Actually, a copy of the *Mona Lisa* that purports to *be* the *Mona Lisa* would be unique.'

" 'Perhaps I will add a mustache to make her more unique.'

" 'You are mocking me.'

" 'Oui! Yes—Tell him, Peter!' shouted the Director.

" 'To answer your question, Vernet,' cooed the collector, 'you would still not be a genius by doing so because you aimed at being a genius. Genius is *unintentional*. It does not aspire. Works of genius are spontaneous. Away with craftsmanship, then! Away with intention and purpose and study and every rule of art! Most of all, be done with realism, and do what is unnatural. Commit anarchy! Half of every painting should be done blindfolded. One should never paint if he thinks he knows how, for knowledge is the enemy. And even so, anyone who believes he is something is certainly not.'

" 'So Caruso is not a great singer if he happens to *think* he is a great singer?' I asked incredulously.

" 'Exactly. No one is that which he thinks he is. There are only a few like me who understand this. But we are not without patience and compassion, Peter. Our goal is to help others understand these new definitions of life and art. To think of the ignorance of art historians over these past centuries! Tsk! Tsk!'

" 'According to your own definition, then, you have no patience, compassion, or understanding, since you think you have these traits.'

" 'You are still mocking me, Vernet! I am merely saying, as Socrates once said, that the only thing I know is that I know nothing.'

" 'At least we agree you know nothing,' said I.

" 'Correct! Even *I* am not what I think—and I think I am a bad man.' Kern's smile broadened into loud raucous laughter.

" 'Or perhaps, Monsieur' I replied, when his guffawing had finally subsided, 'you have just shown your 'genius' by being *unintentionally* correct about being a bad man.'

" 'Such fun, such fun,' muttered Wolfgang Kern as he blew his nose into a handkerchief. 'Some day you will understand, Peter. And everything will be different for you.'

" 'I pray to God, not, sir.'

" 'All this silly talk. How I hate philosophizing! So you are on the North Pole and I on the South. They are both cold and frigid places! Let us meet at the equator in the warm jungles of life! Yes, that is the real world! Your youngest sister, for example—she is in the real world.'

" 'How do you know of my sister?'

" 'Such a lovely child—no? And yet so young to be so crippled.'

" 'How do you know this?' I demanded.

" 'I have studied the jungles, Peter—both real jungles, and the jungles of life. The former is what attracted me to Ryder's work to begin with—his reference to the wildness of Ceylon so evident in his work. Ah, Ceylon—that beautiful pearly toe of India—Verdant! Verdant! *L'amour*! I learned a lesson from that wondrous jungle. There are monkeys captured for pets in Ceylon. They are easy to trick, really. A dried coconut is bored with a hole big enough for a curious monkey to reach his hand inside it to get a nut. But then he finds he cannot withdraw his hand. He is stuck, you see, because he will not let go of the nut, and his fist is too big to fit back through the hole. You, Peter, are the monkey, and the nut inside the coconut is the surgery and braces your young sister will need if she is ever to marry and lead a normal life.'

" 'You are a beast!' cried the Director. 'You will use a little girl to get your way? You are even worse than I imagined!'

"Kern ignored the Director's outburst. 'I sympathize with your family's dilemma, Vernet. I know that your father died three years ago and that your brother is ill. You alone now bear the burdens of your family. Your salary at the Louvre must be a modest one—certainly not one prepared to meet all of life's little contingencies. I am here to help you. As you evidently do not trust me, I will advance to you whatever money your sister's doctor tells me is necessary to have her in braces. There is no risk to you, Peter—a temporary blow to your credibility when the public finds there were swindled—that is all. And they will easily forgive you when they realize you were only trying to recover the *Mona Lisa* and help your sister. What do you say?'

"I tell you, Mr. Holmes, this man's insolence and manipulation were maddening. I was angry, too, that he had inquired into the private matters of my family. I had hardly begun to debate in my mind whether or not I should agree to Kern's plan about the *Mona Lisa* when the Director surprised us all by breaking the silence."

" 'Do it, Peter,' he said, flatly.

" 'What?'

" 'He accepts your offer, Kern. No, do not argue with me, Peter. Kern is right. You are young, and the public will forgive you as soon as your sister's circumstances are known. As for us at the Louvre—well, we are old men. It does not matter. Only the da Vinci matters.' I looked at the Director, but, except for his eyes which glistened, his expression was inscrutable.

"I continued to object, but Mssr. Bantock remained solemn and resolute. As these two antagonists were agreed on nothing else save that I should accept Kern's offer, I decided the plan, however flawed, presented certain advantages that would be lost if I did not agree. And that is why, Holmes, I lent my copy of the *Mona Lisa* to the Louvre to be used at this madman's discretion."

Holmes had remained quietly absorbed in his cousin's peculiar adventure until this last statement, when he gave a moderate outburst of bristling contempt.

"Mad, is he?" exclaimed Holmes. "Mad as a fox watching its prey, I should think! Did Kern ever offer to buy your copy from you?"

"Never."

"Pray, continue."

"I was still hesitant about the plan, Holmes, and delayed the completion of the painting for some little time. But several days ago, after a week of applying a chemical overlay to achieve cracking, and also drying an opaque, sfumato-like glazing onto the painting, the copy was completed and photographed. I then crated up the finished painting. Finally, I went down to the rail station where a ticket had been purchased for me to ride to Eyford, where Ryder's house lay several miles beyond. I was waiting on the wooden platform in a light drizzle for the train's arrival, and wondering what type of man James Ryder would prove to be, when a well-dressed middle-aged man who was wheezing for breath limped heavily toward me.

" 'Are you Peter Vernet?' he gasped.

" 'Yes,' I replied.

" 'I am James Ryder,' said he, grabbing hold of my hand.

Chapter Four

Vernet settled back in this armchair, and a calming influence began to overcome the tone of agitation that had marked the first part of his narrative. He took another drink of water to sooth his parched throat, then set the tumbler down next to him on the table and placed his elbows on the arms of his chair. Holmes, Miss Ryder, and I all waited impatiently for him to continue his remarkable narrative.

"Well, Holmes," said he at last, "the unexpected epiphany of J. Leslie Ryder, this short and coarse-looking man best known for his unconventional paintings and for that small, but fanatical, band of admirers who champion his cause, took me absolutely by surprise. 'I didn't expect to see you here, Mr. Ryder,' I said. 'I was told to bring my painting to your estate.'

" 'You're right,' he replied, 'but I'm not used to doctor's orders, and I don't care much for being locked up in my own house, however big it is. I took an earlier train so that we could discuss some matters in private. I also don't care for my agent to know all my business, Vernet, and you come highly recommended by the Director. Ah, here is the train now.'

"The great, black, iron behemoth strained against its screeching breaks, and billowing clouds of steam erupted from its boiler-driven smokestack as the train pulled into the station. A sparse amount of folk began boarding.

" 'That will be our coach,' said Ryder, pointing to one of the cars. 'No, I won't mind if you smoke. The doctor thought I should smoke myself in hopes of clearing the lungs. It's a popular theory, you know. Gets rid of the debris, I'm told. I'll try anything at this point.' "

Sherlock Holmes held up his hand. "Just a moment, Vernet. How would you describe the appearance of James Ryder?"

"Well, I would say his coat was a simple one—gray, with a thick winter blend of finely textured—"

"No, no—I mean his physicality and personal projection."

"Oh that! Well, he struck me as a shrimp of a fellow, really, not much taller than myself! Average weight for his short height. But he had a long face that accentuated his peering expression, and there was a slight bow to him, as though he were bearing some great weight upon his shoulders. Otherwise, there was an average amount of hair on his head, if the same could not be said of his goatee, which was, in fact, invisible from a distance, and a poor excuse for what seems to pass these days as an identification badge for artists. As for the man's personality, I would say he spoke forthrightly about a great many things, yet he could be deferring when he wanted. I came to reflect afterward that he might be aware of a certain naiveté in his own nature, but seems to have embraced it rather than to have lived a diffident life."

"I assume you never met Ryder before?"

"Never."

"Holmes looked puzzled. In the main, your physical description agrees with what I know of him. But the personality is somewhat different. Please go on."

Well, Holmes, I decided to follow Ryder onto the train, if for no other reason than to carry the painting for him, for he appeared to have an asthmatic condition and showed signs of strain. Our journey began with a lurch from the train, and with another belch from the single volcanic nostril of the locomotive, and soon we were on our way. By the end of the first half-hour of our conversation we had passed the last dun-coloured brick buildings that marked the Eastern outstretch of the great city, and before us lay an early spring landscape of trees and bushes in early bloom. Ryder spoke of his interest in native English plants and trees, and his knowledge was surprisingly remarkable. However one might despise his art, I decided this man was no buffoon. Of course, my interest in Ryder was somewhat piqued by the strong contrast of feelings exchanged by Kern and Bantok some time before, and which capstoned for me the rumors that for years have flown around the Louvre about Ryder's life and art. On the whole, though, I found Ryder gentler in disposition than one might have thought. He seemed nervous, I'll grant you that, but I saw nothing in his manner that hinted at an extravagant nature, or at some eccentricity in his personality that explained the bizarre nature of his art. Only in his manner of dress was there a glimpse of the purse that afforded the original oils of various Masters I would later see hanging in the hallway of his villa.

"Our conversation about art began awkwardly at first, for we are in different schools within the art world and could not be more different in style and philosophy. Yet any of his constraint in conversation I finally marked down to certain bodily pains that caused him to frequently wince during our interview. We soon found a mutual sympathy, however, when Ryder abruptly announced his feelings for his agent.

" 'What do you think of that scoundrel, Kern?' remarked Ryder.

" 'I'm surprised at your description!' I replied.

" 'Yes! I suppose I *was* being generous,' said he, laughing. 'I should have referred to him as that *clever and dangerous* scoundrel.'

" 'I don't understand, Monsieur. If you feel this way, why does he represent you?'

Vernet tipped his hat upon meeting Ryder

" 'Why, indeed?' said he, half-shrugging his shoulders and puffing thoughtfully on his cigarette. 'I suppose there are a couple of reasons, Vernet. First of all, he is a salesman who is very good at what he does. Only a superb salesman could maneuver himself into running a coup against the Director of the Louvre. He loves this idea of being the next *enfant terrible* of the art world. I've observed him for some years, now. I think his full goal, unknown even to himself, is to be accepted by those old-world bearers of aristocratic taste that he claims to despise. He hopes to win them over with his charm, but if not, well, he would be equally glad to achieve a position in the Louvre that would strike fear in their hearts. That is Kern. He needs a unique plan to do this, and has this idea of flushing the *Mona Lisa* out from its hiding place. His ambition is great, and is only exceeded by his consuming passions for money and women—he thinks of these all the time, and for him, money and women are acquisitions—nothing more—the former attracting the latter, and both to be used at his will. All his goals begin with this lustful desire for money. And every salesman like he wants the mother lode—some unique product that no other salesman has. That is where my art comes into the picture. He needs my art, and I need his salesmanship. He is the horse, and I am the wagon full of produce—subtract either one and the fruit will not get to the market. We both realize that our fortunes and hopes for immortality are dependent upon each other's talents.'

" 'You speak rather frankly.'

" 'Every artist longs for immortality, Vernet. Surely you know that. Everything will fall into place once Kern's plan has runs its course. You have not realized, have you, that in his daring plan to flush out the *Mona Lisa* with your forgery Kern is acting as your salesman as well? Even your own fortune and immortality are tied to him. Now don't look so disgusted! I'm glad, at least, that this realization has only now struck you, for it speaks of your innocence and naiveté in all this sordid world. Well, so much for that!'

" 'And that is why he represents you, because of his salesmanship?'

" 'Primarily so.'

" 'You mentioned some additional reason, too.'

" 'Oh, that is much more painful for me to speak about. This other reason concerns my weakness.'

" 'You mean your physical weakness?'

" 'Not at all, though it's true I haven't had my legs and stomach for some months, and these fevers will be the death of me. Had it not been for Kern's energy of late, my introduction to the Louvre would have been in jeopardy. Self-promotion at this critical time has been impossible for me with so little strength. But that's not the weakness I'm referring to.'

" 'What, then?'

" 'The weakness of a man to put his own fame and fortune above the good of his family. To 'follow one's star', to 'insist on one's self', as Emerson says. I did this, Vernet—I embraced myself. And I refused to listen to those who told me how costly it would be. My wife and children were the first casualties of my vision, but how little it concerned me then! What do you think, Vernet? Was it I at fault, or the artist in me?'

" 'I'm sure I could not say.'

" 'I don't think there is any difference between the two. Have you thought upon this problem? How many artists do you suppose remain faithful to their family, especially their wives, throughout their entire artistic life? That's right, practically none! Our selfishness drives them away—the kind that insists on loyalty to art above all other affections. And even when we artists do not leave our wives and children we often feel alienated and divorced from other things—from a world that does not understand us, or from our own art over which we entertain many a private doubt. Many trials face the artist, Vernet, but, for us, a painter's life is the supreme calling. Indeed, you know the old saying, 'The artist thanks God for his fate, and that everyone else is spared it.' "

" 'Yes, I have heard that.'

" 'I finally see that artists have this incredible selfishness about them. That is their weakness; they hardly care about anything besides their own selves and their art. They even imagine that this selfishness is their strength! I realize all this now and have begun to change. I think more about the interests of others, and less about myself. For example, I have come to my daughter's aid for the first time in thirteen years. I recently found that scheming fellow Kern rummaging through my correspondence one day, apparently trying to figure out the identity of a woman whose photograph had gotten separated from its letter. I demanded to know what he was doing, and he told me. But far from being ashamed he was in a rare fit, obsessed with the beauty of the woman, and he even spoke of the shameful things he planned for her. I surprised him by telling him it was my daughter, and that he would stand clear or suffer the consequences. He was astonished at the fact, or at my boldness—I'm not sure which—and has not bothered me about it since, though of course, I worry now about what he has learned, for he is a *collector*. But here is her picture. Look for yourself, Vernet. Tell me she is not beautiful.'

"I looked at the photograph, and indeed, her beauty was most unusual. 'It is not hard to imagine how a man might be smitten with her,' I said.

" 'Yes, I knew you would think so, Vernet. You have the artist's eye.'

Holmes and I watched Vernet as he momentarily interrupted his account to glance awkwardly in the direction of Miss Ryder. She, in turn, sat coquettishly in her chair and received the compliment without giving a hint of her own feelings. Holmes gave a slight roll of his eyes as one consigned to a room where the torture consisted of having to endure the telling of some yellow back novel. "Please, Vernet," said Holmes, who had been wholly occupied with the story up to this point, "tell us the remainder of your conversation with James Ryder."

"Of course. "Where was I? Oh, yes, Ryder had mentioned my artistic eye. Then he spoke of his business partner. 'Kern is easily bored and fickle in his tastes,' said he, 'whether it be women or art. Six months ago it was the Italians, now it is the Spanish, tomorrow it will be the Dutch.'

" 'Do you mean women or art?'

" 'Art,' he replied with a laugh.

" 'Oh, I know he likes the Spanish for the moment,' I said, 'for the Director lent him an instrument so he could take a paint sample from a Velasquez. It will make certain the painting's age.'

" 'To determine its authenticity?'

" 'Exactly.'

" 'I didn't know that was possible.'

" 'Yes, the blue paint used by Velasquez was made from powdered lapis lazuli stones. The blue used today contains ferrocyanide of iron, discovered around 1700 but not publicly marketed until the 1780s. Many of Velasquez' paintings date from the decades surrounding the 1660s, so any blue paint found to have ferrocyanide of iron cannot come from a Velasquez.'

" 'How interesting,' remarked Ryder. "So an analysis of blue paint can sometimes reveal a forgery.'

" 'Yes, and chemists have been analyzing certain reds, as well. But please come to me, not the Director, if you have any questions about authenticity in your own collections. I was embarrassed to have to tell Kern that the Director was wrong about the tested sample needing to be green. Of course, I didn't correct the Director in his presence.'

" 'You say Kern was loaned an instrument for this?'

" 'A hypodermic syringe.'

"Ryder gave a worried look. 'I know that Kern once struggled with the cocaine habit. I will have to keep watching him, for I have noticed a recent excitability in him. Perhaps it is for the drug, or perhaps it is for my daughter. Either way it will prove bad for me.'

" 'Is there nothing you can do to protect your daughter?'

" 'I will warn her when I see her in a few days. But beautiful women like Rachel often attract the wrong type of men. Take my wife for example. When she was young, she was as beautiful as my daughter, and yet she ended up with me!'

" 'And after your marriage you felt unsuitable for it?'

" 'Yes, though I stayed with my wife for some time. But eventually I became restless. I wanted to experience more of life, more of art, more of everything! I left her when a woman's beauty could no longer hold me. I want to speak frankly with you, Vernet. I have a premonition that I may not live much longer. You seem to be a man of sense and discretion, and I need someone with whom I can speak intimately of my affairs. You see, there may be some inquiries about my life and art when I am gone, and Kern is too much the fool to know how to answer for me. Only a man of sense can make an explanation to posterity.'

" 'I trust your fears about your future are unfounded, sir."

" 'So you would think,' said the man as he looked at me in a searching way. 'Yes,' he said, 'I do think you are the man to hear my story.'

" 'Then I would be honoured,' I replied.

"The man lay back in his tartan-cloth seat and his ear slowly cocked to a position as though the monotonous rumble of train wheels over the rail joints would somehow bring up the full sentiment of his life's memories.

'Well,' he began, 'the first thing to tell you is that my life took a wrong turn early, and I was always in trouble as a boy. Yet once I was grown, I believed I had conquered my irresponsibility, and I took a wife. But I found that after a decade of marriage the desire for other things held me in greater spell than my matrimonial vows. I experimented with this vision. I was reckless at first, foolish and impatient. I nearly lost my freedom in a bungled attempt at stealing a priceless stone called the Blue Carbuncle—you've probably heard of it. I was given a reprieve by the detective, Sherlock Holmes, but rather than reform my ways I considered more carefully the goals I wished to obtain. I wanted money and renown—*yes*—to have my name fixed among the great men of this world! As I thought upon these aims a plan took shape in my mind. I had read about Gaugin when I was younger and was compelled by his flight into a primitive world. I now studied him more carefully to learn the reason for his success. I came to a conclusion: his paintings were average, but his promiscuity sold. People loved speculating about his South Sea exploits and his bohemian ways. The exotic setting where he lived and painted helped him to rise above the colourless crowd of other artists. He grew to command great prices for his paintings as his notoriety increased. He had his cake, and ate it, too.

" 'Having studied Gaugin, I realized my art, too, would need a similar response if I were to be successful. My life would be a forgery, Vernet, nothing more. I would have to attract an audience by giving them what they wanted, and they, in turn, would sing my praises. Not just an audience made up of young, progressive-thinking people who had no influence with the editors of newspapers and curators of galleries. No, my audience would also include stodgy old men tired of their conventional lives and lifeless marriages—men ready enough to express their vicarious rebellion by supporting my art. England I judged as too prudish for such an audience, but France seemed a fertile soil. After all, they had already shown an affection for Gaugin. To double-check my conclusion about the French, I studied some of their literature, especially the kind that comments on society. Gustave Flaubert seemed to be the leading critic among the French, so I read his books. I found he despaired in particular about the decadence of the middle class. These were words I needed to hear. I rejoiced in how the French could be blasé and titillated at the same time. The more disgust Flaubert expressed, the gladder I became, for I hoped this same class of society would embrace one more wanderer. Of course I would paint different than Gaugin; cruder and stupider, and more reckless. But it might just lead to success.'

" 'I packed my things and left for Ceylon, and soon found that the wayward life came natural to me. Kern arrived a month or so after my arrival. He's actually a distant relative of my wife. We became friends, and to pass the time he made up stories for the public prints in Europe about my supposed love for those French decadent Romantics like Jean Jacque Rousseau, especially the drivel about my wanting a primitive life and morality. It was all wonderfully calculated. Through the years Kern has provided many good stories to the newspapers.' "

" 'So your life on Ceylon was unlike your reputation?'

" 'Oh, no, much of it was true. I led the happy and hedonistic life people expected me to. Not until a year-and-a-half ago did the island become unbearable for me.'

" 'Something happened to you?' "

" 'Yes—a very terrible circumstance. One day I was painting on a high cliff overlooking the shore, enjoying as always the warmth of the sun and the restful sound of sea waves crashing against the distant rocks. Over the years I had met a native woman and established a kind of family on the island, shameful by any English standards, but a son, nonetheless, and one I delighted in. These two had waded out to a sandbar several hundred yards away to collect shells. On such occasions they usually returned after a few hours, but this time they delayed, probably because the shells were very plentiful due to a recent equinoctial storm. A strong wind and menacing clouds blew up suddenly, however, and a storm broke down upon the beach and aggravated the already rising tide to a point where the ocean began reclaiming the sandbar. It all happened at once. I saw the boy on his mother's shoulders clutching his bag of shells with one hand and holding on to her with the other, while she stood on the sandbar in waist-deep water. I sensed trouble, and ran toward the path that led down from the cliff. I could see her carefully step off into the waves in the direction of the shore. The turgid waters rolled about her head, and a breath at the wrong moment would have meant disaster for them both. Her native sense seemed as though it would prevail, however, and I saw that she was slowly gaining the shore, taking a few steps each time the trough of a wave allowed her feet to touch the ocean floor. But without warning, a huge breaker knocked them over into the violence of the deep surf. My son became caught in a strong rip-tide current that sucked his body beyond the sandbar, and his mother swam frantically after him. I hoped to rescue them, but by the time I scrambled down from the last rocks and ran into the ocean they had already been swept away. Quite some distance from me two other islanders had also seen the boy and his mother carried out, and had run along the beach and into the raging waters behind me. After a long and agonizing search for some hours, it was evident the boy and his mother were gone forever.

That terrible event is why I left the island, Vernet. I searched my soul often in the months that followed their deaths. There are not many men in this life with whom God returns an eye for an eye, but I am one of them. I had abandoned my family in England, including a son I never knew. I am told he died because his mother was too poor to get him proper medical treatment. I recently learned of his fate from my daughter's letters. Had I remained in England things might have turned out different, but instead I lived the life of a colonial with a concubine. I don't tell you these things to gain sympathy from you, Vernet, but only because I want my experiences to help someone like yourself avoid the same kind of mistakes. The life of an artist is so precarious, you know.'

"Ryder then leaned forward in his seat and gazed out the coach window. The timeworn lines in his face and the faraway look in his eyes told of his many trials. We talked further, and he spoke wistfully of his daughter—yes, you, Miss Ryder—whom he greatly admires, and how he wished he had been a better father. I tell you, Holmes, had you been with me, you too would have sensed a tragic figure in this man.

"Are you saying," queried Holmes, "that for all his shortcomings Ryder was honest about his failures?"

"Yes, and I even ventured to tell him so."

"What was his response?"

"He gave a grunt. 'Regret won't get me back my family,' he said."

"You believe he genuinely saw his past as a failure, then?"

"Yes, except for his art."

"And what of his present and future? What does he think these hold for him?"

"His eyes grew bright at one point as he spoke excitedly about his plans to visit America where he hoped for a new beginning. He admitted the distance would stifle his renewed acquaintance with his daughter, but was convinced she was better off without him. He is afraid his reputation has already hurt her own chances to get commissions in London where most work is sponsored by a conservative philanthropy devoted to religious causes.

"Besides being nervous about meeting his daughter in London in a few days, the chief thing that seemed to occupy his mind was his condition for his overseas trip. I asked him why his health had declined. He believes his body has suffered since he left the tropical Indian breezes for the damp and cooler climate of England. He is often weak and feverish, and he has a certain lethargy that he blames on his sickness, though apparently his doctor views the full matter of his health as more of a mystery.

" 'It's my legs that worry me most,' he said, as our train began slowing down. 'Some days they feel like pillars of stone, and I can hardly move them. I have nausea, too, and headaches throughout the day.'

" 'What treatment does your doctor suggest?' I asked.

" 'He says to follow the biblical injunction and take a little wine for the stomach's sake.' Ryder smiled. 'I make sure I do.'

"On the whole, Holmes, I could not help feeling some pity for this man. He believes his paintings have an historical value, which is pathetic in itself, for they are, as the Director says, like the mere scribblings of a child. Indeed, he is a little squirrel of a man, hardly the kind you would suspect could cause this notorious stir among women that we read of in the papers. They dote on him much more than the men, so much, in fact, that he is glad to have a man as forceful as Kern to champion his works before the male critics of newspapers and the members of the Louvre."

"I suppose," remarked Holmes, "that the purchase of Ryder's work would be a first of its kind at the Louvre."

"Yes. But such a collection would delight the younger members to the same degree that it would horrify the old guard, and there is no common ground between these groups. If the collection is bought, the older members who control such purchases plan on selling it to the d' Orsay for a few works of Delacroix and Courbet, who now look like saints compared to Ryder."

"I see," replied Holmes. "Please continue."

"By this time the train had arrived at our station, and a driver transferred our bags and the crated painting to a dogcart. It was a half-hour's ride to Ryder's villa, and when we arrived Ryder gave me a short tour of his estate. Designed in a conglomeration of architectural styles, the large ivy-covered building was impressive, but in need of considerable repair. I marveled at the difference of the interior, however, which was well maintained, and which had been richly furnished a century before by local artisans who had cut the house's furniture from a variety of woods gained in the surrounding forest. However, of all the furnishings and decorations in the house Ryder was most proud of his collection of paintings. He had put a few of them in his city suite, but brought most of them to the country where he spent most of his time. The paintings consisted of mostly lesser-known works by important British artists, such as Constable, Reynolds, Blake, and Turner.

"We ended the tour of his house in the library, where we spoke at length, especially of the personal consequences we each risked in co-operating with Kern's plan. We agreed that a recovery of the *Mona Lisa* would go a long way toward mitigating any sacrifice on our parts. The conversation was winding down and, noting the time and the rail schedule, I rose to leave. Then suddenly Ryder grabbed my sleeve.

" 'I want to ask you something before you go,' said he, holding my arm and peering at me with curiosity. 'Is it true,' he asked, 'that you are a cousin of Sherlock Holmes?'

" 'Yes, it is,' I replied.

" 'I should like to speak to him as soon as possible.'

" 'He is at his old address,' I answered. Suddenly I realized my *faux pas* in recalling his interrogation at your hands, Holmes. 'Not that you would know where that is—' I added.

"Ryder laughed goodheartedly. 'I'm not offended, Vernet. It was at those apartments that I got a second chance. For a long time I made a mess of it. Yes, I want to see him. But I feel so terribly sick. Please tell him I *must* see him—this week if possible.'

" 'I will telegram him tomorrow.'

" 'No, please—on second thought I would prefer that you go in person. The request will seem more earnest that way. Take your leave from work by making what excuse you can. Here,' said he, urging me to take money, 'I will pay you a fortnight's wages for your inconvenience. The matter is a most urgent one. I simply *must* see Holmes.' He pressed the matter so earnestly that I was compelled to accept his demands and generosity. 'If only Holmes knew the exact nature of my affairs,' said he, 'he would come at once.' Then pointing to a dusty fiddle in the corner, he added, 'Should anything overtake me in Paris before Holmes visits me, tell him to please give this violin to my daughter. This instrument is the most precious possession I have. It may not be the finest made, but it has provided me with many moments of comfort through the years. Holmes will understand.'

" 'But why not give her the violin yourself? You'll see her in just a few days.'

" 'I hope to. But if not, Holmes must be the one. He too is a violinist and will stand in my stead if I am unable to.' Then clutching a lapel of my coat Ryder said in a desperate tone, 'Tell Holmes I love the sound of a violin. The violin is the end of music for me. Will you tell Holmes I said so?'

" 'What exactly?'

" *'That the violin is the end of music for me.'*

" 'Certainly, if you wish it.'

" 'Those exact words.'

" 'Of course.'

" 'I cannot thank you enough, then.'

"Ryder fell back into his chair and gasped for breath. This last effort to speak required such strength of conviction that he now looked totally exhausted. In a feeble voice he congratulated me on my painting and assured me its excellence would make the whole plan for recovering the da Vinci possible. He looked forward to the autumn when the plan would begin immediately after his departure for America. But I tell you, Holmes, I had a black foreboding as I left his house."

"A foreboding of what?"

"I'm not sure, really. Perhaps I was troubled to have to relay his message to you. I think he believed he would never see you."

"Did he mention anyone else during your conversation?"

"Not more than a passing reference, at least."

"Who was it?"

"He mentioned his wife in a round about way."

"Details! Details!" cried my companion.

"You are relentless, Holmes," said Vernet with an amused look of appeal. "Very well. When Ryder wrote to his daughter, he mentioned his illness. She, in turn, told her mother, who insisted that a certain physician be called. Mrs. Ryder believed her husband had been out of the country too many years to be properly familiar with any doctors."

"That was rather kind."

"I thought so, too. Ryder accepted his wife's recommendation and asked the doctor to come. Mrs. Ryder heard of it and decided to accompany the doctor to see her husband. She rode as far as the druggist's, where the doctor left the cab to get some medicine. But she was gone from the carriage when the doctor returned."

"You say she left the carriage *before* the doctor returned from the druggist's?"

"Yes."

"Did she leave with the doctor any gifts of food or drink to be forwarded to her husband?"

"From what Ryder told me of his conversation with the doctor, I would say she did not."

"And what reason did she give the doctor in order that she might accompany him in the first place? I trust not many women would be so forthcoming as to visit a husband to forgive him for a decade of infidelity."

"She said she wished to discuss her daughter's future with Ryder."

"That would be natural enough, I suppose. Yet her nerve failed her. Why, I wonder? Most women are formidable where their children are concerned."

"I know something of women, Holmes. I believe an ill humor overtook her on the way as she reflected on all the misery that Ryder had caused her. Such feelings would naturally affect her spirit during an interview. As her daughter's future was at stake she decided to postpone the meeting."

"That is certainly possible," remarked Holmes, "though I prefer more data before coming to a conclusion. But how coincidental our thoughts! I was just telling Miss Ryder last night that I, too, know something of women. There is no doubt, though, that I should benefit from a conversation with Mrs. Ryder."

"And what can be done about James Ryder sitting in jail, Holmes?"

"I will tell Lestrade to speak to you of the matter. It may take a day or two, but if there is innocence in this man, he can be released. If you will excuse us, Vernet, Dr. Watson and I shall escort Miss Ryder home. I would like to get Mrs. Ryder's view on the whole matter as soon as possible."

We all rose, and Vernet looked at Rachel Ryder with an indecisive yet tender look in his eyes. "*Adieu*, and good-day, Mademoiselle."

"You don't realize it, Mssr. Vernet," said Miss Ryder, "but I saw your copy of the *Mona Lisa* at the Louvre when it was nearly finished. I was struck by its perfection. No wonder that you have the confidence of the Director and Mssr. Kern. I am so glad to have finally met you."

"The pleasure is mine," stammered Vernet, as he tried to gather his wits. "Perhaps," said he, "some day your mother could escort you to the theatre with me?" Then, quitting any remnant of caution, Vernet blurted out, "Please, someday you will let me paint your portrait, too, Mademoiselle. No?"

"What on earth for?"

"Your beauty, Mademoiselle. That I may never be without it. That I may never lack for inspiration."

Miss Ryder blushed, momentarily speechless before the impetuous Frenchman. "I—I will ask Mother," she replied. "I think she would allow that."

For a brief moment Vernet stood still, shocked by his good fortune. Then he gave a little bow and waved his hand with an awkward flourish. "Till to-morrow, then," he said with nervous delight, and he grabbed our coats and handed them to us with as much dignity as this comic moment would allow.

Such, I thought, were the beginnings of love.

Chapter Five

Our carriage ride to Mrs. Ryder's house was a cold and bitter one. Holmes drew his coat about him and seemed oblivious to the howling winds that rattled the windows and shook the cab. With his chin upon his breast and the brim of his hat pulled over his eyes he remained silent during the entire ride, quite aloof, it seemed, from his surroundings. I, on the other hand, could practically feel and hear in the outside screaming air a faraway echo of all the wailing misery expressed by the Ryder women during those past years when they faced death and hardship. I imagined, too, in the heightened pitch of gusts pounding against the sides of the carriage, the repentant cries of James Ryder (if Ryder it be!), the man responsible for all this misery, heeding at last to that warning once given by a first-century apostle and now reaching him after echoing down through two-score generations of preachers: 'Howl and weep, rich man, for your misery shall come upon you.' I wondered, too, if Ryder might have read that other proverb quoted in last month's *Times* by one of London's more colourful preachers, a maxim which seemed so apropos to his vagabond life, i.e., that there were many ways a man could desert his family, and any of them made him worse than an infidel. All these winds of grief now seemed to come together outside our carriage window to demand an answer, each a thread shaded with the pathos of life and woven into some textile of flawed tapestry in chaotic design.

Through Eastgate we rode, then past the Tunwell Bridge and on to Fugard's Lane, an alley hardly fitting the mood of our journey to-day, for it was a lovely lane and one lined with gardens that back small pleasant cottages maintained by their squired owners or by younger sons from aristocratic families who had not the fortune of primogeniture. A further drive of twenty minutes brought us to the poorer south end of London, where after some narrow turns down rutty streets we finally arrived at Mrs. Ryder's home. Departing from the carriage, we saw before us a short lawn that ended at an uneven arboretum hedge. Beyond this stood a house, a one-story affair of yellow brick and stone lentils with the kind of long narrow single-casement windows facing the street that caused wintry draughts in blustery weather. Azalea bushes marked the spaces between the windows, and were the singular exception among the botanicals that had been pruned. We went up the walk of angular limestone, cracked and worn smooth by generations of past inhabitants; a pavement where on one side stood a dogwood in bloom, and on the other a weathered oak, limbless and truncated from disease. I could not help but think how the condition of these trees seemed to represent the Ryder family in its different phases over the years.

In the next moment we entered the foyer of the house which quickly opened to a brightly lit drawing room with French double doors leading to the outside. This space apparently doubled as the library, having several bookshelves against one wall. The room's most striking feature, however, and one that stood in stark contrast to the otherwise plain furnishings of the room (there was no bric-a-brac nor even photos to be seen), was a group of splendid paintings hung high upon the walls. Rachel Ryder left to call her mother, and while she was gone

Holmes looked closely at the plentiful assortment of books and with a splayed hand rubbed his fingertips over some of the best spines in admiration of the bindings.

"I see that Mrs. Ryder is a persevering woman who values education," said he.

I looked at the amount of worn books and imagined someone trying to read them all. "I gather, Holmes, that you deduce both facts from the used appearance of so many books."

"Yes, Watson, and her love of books can also be seen in the disproportional amount of money she has spent on them rather than on the furniture which is quite plain."

Holmes resumed his survey of the volumes, leafing through a set about Napoleon, a bound-in year of medical journals, and some books for children. From there he inspected the paintings, and was in the midst of drawing my attention to his tactile inspection of the scrolled framework of several pictures when Miss Ryder returned to introduce her mother.

Elisabeth Ryder was a beautiful woman approaching middle age whose form and face was akin to the beauty of her daughter. She was tall, and upon entering the room she stopped and stood before us in a ballerina-like pose with her feet touching at an angle so that one foot was placed slightly in front of the other, with the fingers of her hands intertwined, and with her arms bent slightly at the elbows. A blue dress graced the lines of her remarkable figure, and I thought how odd the human species was to produce a man like James Ryder who had found other attractions greater than that for which another man might certainly die. I found Ryder's desertion even more inconceivable when I realized Mrs. Ryder was thirteen years younger when he left her. Then again, there was always the woman's personality to consider. At any rate, I was not surprised that the woman's equilibrium was tried by our unexpected arrival, and she made no effort to hide her annoyance.

"And who do I have the pleasure of meeting at so *unexpected* an hour?" she inquired.

"I am Sherlock Holmes. And this is my friend, Doctor Watson. The matter is a most urgent one, Madame."

"You are the one who freed my criminal husband so many years ago?"

"I deeply apologize, Madame."

The woman compressed her lips before replying, but a brief elevation of her cheekbones told me that she had momentarily clenched her teeth. "My daughter believes I can help you in regards to my husband, Mr. Holmes," said she. "I do not see how, but you may ask me your questions, so long as you note that I have an appointment within an hour."

"Thank you Mrs. Ryder. I will only take a moment. Are you currently seeking reconciliation with your husband?"

The woman gave a start and laughed bitterly. "Certainly not. Whatever gave you that idea?"

"I was merely inquiring."

"My goodness, you get to it, Mr. Holmes! You certainly mince words!"

"I leave poetry to others, Madame."

"Yes, apparently. What am I seeking, you ask? I am seeking *justice,* Mr. Holmes. Most particularly for my daughter who grew up without a father. He abandoned her while she was still a child. Had it not been for my own father, we would have made our bed on the cobblestones, you can be sure of that."

"Your father has been of some help to you, then?"

"Yes. And while we're on the subject of finance, Rachel told me of some money you gave her in lieu of a violin. That was certainly generous. May I assume there is no obligation of any sort owed to you for this gentlemanly kindness?"

"None owed, whatsoever."

The lady searched my companion's face with skepticism, seeking some hint of hidden betrayal. At length she relaxed her composure a little.

"Now Madame," continued Holmes, "I understand that you accompanied the doctor on his way to see your husband."

"That is correct."

"Why did you leave the carriage at the druggist's?"

"I felt a nervous sickness on the way and had to return home."

"Why did you want to see him?"

"It was for Rachel's sake that I went. In recent months her paintings have attracted the attention of some notable persons. They have urged her to travel abroad to Italy to further her understanding of art, but her scholarship does not cover such expenses. My father has often helped us, but he had a bad blow in the stocks recently. Rachel felt she could earn the money herself by doing family chores at a professor's home. But when I estimated the amount normally paid to a maid for such work and compared it to the actual cost of university tuition, it became apparent to me that one might be expected to perform other duties than just washing the linens. At the very least I believed there was an appearance of compromise. My daughter dismissed my feelings, saying a friend of hers had taken such a position and was none the less for it. But I don't trust the homes of professors. Men spending all day thinking instead of working. Oh, *pardon* me, Mr. Holmes.

"Anyway, when I heard that my husband had returned to England Rachel and I were at loggerheads, for I had decided his purse should be a resource for Rachel. My husband's pursuit of art, or what he imagines is art, left our children without him, and with no real means to live. Our son had died during his absence, and there was only our daughter to consider. Why should James begrudge her a few coppers for all the misery he had caused? I steeled myself for an interview with him. Then, to my surprise, Rachel suddenly desired to communicate with her father. She also discouraged me from seeing him, for our feelings are very opposite toward him, and she feared I might put him off. For several weeks I consented, but after some correspondence was exchanged between them I decided it was time to call upon him.

"Before my intended visit, however, James became quite sick and was in need of a doctor. I told Rachel to recommend to James a specialist that my father knows, a Dr. Stenerude, known for treating nervous disorders and stomach related diseases. I have used him myself. I asked if I might go with him to see my husband. He agreed and said it would not interfere with his treatment."

Holmes glanced at me with a raised eyebrow, and I returned the look of recognition that the name of Dr. Stenerude commands in London.

"And why the sudden interest in your husband's health, Mrs. Ryder, since by your own admission you feel embittered toward him."

"I wouldn't have him die owing Rachel a chance at life, Mr. Holmes, even if that life were an artistic one. I can think of better things to do with one's life than to paint silly pictures, and always told James that, too. But if that's what Rachel wants to do, then that's what she'll have!"

"I think her ambition is well placed, Madame," commented Holmes as he pointed to the paintings above his head, "For these are all very marvelous. That one in the corner with Napoleon on horseback is equally wonderful, though I believe the palette and brushwork are a little different than the rest."

"You are the first to notice the difference, Mr. Holmes, but you are right. All but that one were painted by my daughter. In fact, I did the Emperor on horseback myself."

"Really? You paint, then, too?"

"I did—long ago, at least. I no longer have the desire. I'm not sure why painting seems so trivial, now. Still, I hate dishonesty even in trivial things, and you've seen my husband's work—all charlatanism and pig slop! I'm surprised that Mssr. Bantock of the Louvre speaks somewhat approvingly of it in the paper. No, the artistic line that runs through Rachel has come through my father's side of the family. I think James was always jealous of that."

"I see. Incidentally, you have been misled about Director Bantock's true feelings. My cousin is a direct witness to the fact that though the Director demonstrates before the public a certain openness toward the latest art trends, he privately detests them. In fact, he truly hates your husband's work. But he avoids controversy because his retirement is at hand."

"He's retiring, then?"

"You didn't know?"

"Not at all. What will the Louvre do without him? Mssr. Bantock *is* the Louvre."

"How remarkable! Quite remarkable, indeed," replied Holmes, as he looked keenly at Mrs. Ryder. "So you've given up the brush and smock. Did you ever replace your interest in painting with something else?"

"I took to reading again which I have often loved. Even as a child history and biography were my favorites."

"Of course—Napoleon and French military history, for example."

"Exactly. Unfortunately, I have no one with whom to share these interests. My daughter thinks history is a bore."

"The young often do. But when reading, Madame, is it your habit to read the last book in a set before its first, as you do the last page of a newspaper before the headlines?"

Mrs. Ryder looked puzzled. "What do you mean?"

"You read newspapers beginning with the back page, do you not?"

"Why do you think—"

"You are aware of Bantock's public statements on the *avant garde*, but not his announcement about his retirement. Of the four major newspapers I read today, only the *Times* mention

Bantock in any way. The *Times* is so driven toward *détente*, you know, especially in view of the German situation, so there is always some French news to be had. Bantock's statement about art was on the back page, his retirement announcement on the front. You were aware of the one, but not of the other. Therefore you read newspapers in reverse order of pagination as many good folk do. My question is whether this habit of yours extends to sets of books."

This whirlwind of deduction took Mrs. Ryder by surprise, and she tightened her composure.

"You're mistaken, Mr. Holmes. I simply glanced at the back page of the newspaper as it lay upon the table."

"You really cannot tell me," asked my friend, pointing to a four volume set of books on a nearby shelf, "if you ignored reading the first three books in this Napoleon set and read the last one only?" As Holmes spoke he pulled from off the shelf a leather-backed, red-paneled volume with a '4' on the ribbed spine and held it in front of her. The colour drained from Mrs. Ryder's face.

"Is this merely a hypothetical example of yours, Mr. Holmes?" She hesitated, but Holmes's commanding demeanor told her his question had been a rhetorical one. 'No, I suppose it's not," she murmured. Another moment of silence passed with Mrs. Ryder in the greatest concentration. "I may have started with the last volume," said she, carefully crafting her words, "I'm having trouble remembering. Ah—yes! I recall what happened now, Mr. Holmes. I had read the first three volumes early last summer while away at Cheltenham to visit my sister, but failed to read the fourth before returning to London to resume my teaching in the fall. I only got to the last volume in recent weeks."

"About the time you contacted the doctor?"

"I really don't remember. But I'm catching on to you, Mr. Holmes. Perhaps you noticed that the first three volumes have a greater amount of dust on the spine. That's why you asked me, isn't it?"

"Perhaps I did notice. Thank you Mrs. Ryder, your explanation is a perfectly natural one."

"Anything else, then? I am due for an appointment."

"Just one question. A cousin of mine says that James Ryder's business partner, Mr. Wolfgang Kern, has a romantic interest in your daughter. Have you ever met this man, Kern?"

The lady hesitated as though Holmes had uttered some unfathomable thought. "No," she replied, "though I have heard the name. I believe he has been mentioned along with my husband in some of the newspaper articles lately. But no such person has been to the house." Mrs. Ryder looked with amused curiosity at her daughter. "Someone has an interest in Rachel? Why should that be suspicious, Mr. Holmes? You see for yourself how beautiful she is. I shouldn't wonder that she has admirers. Now go to the door and see who that is, Rachel."

While Mrs. Ryder had been speaking there had been a frantic knock on the door. To our great surprise it turned out to be Inspector Lestrade of Scotland Yard. This would prove to be the last case of Sherlock Holmes in which Lestrade would ever be involved. Shortly afterward he retired from the force due to unusual circumstances. And though the Yard regretted his departure, for he was among their most experienced men, nothing this day prepared Lestrade to find Holmes and I at Mrs. Ryder's house. He expressed considerable astonishment.

"I certainly didn't expect to see you here, Mr. Holmes. But this will save me a trip to Baker Street. James Ryder is calling for you. He claims to know you."

"Yes, and I was told he was arrested for theft yesterday."

"He's not well," said Lestrade, taking off his cap and holding it between his hands as he stood before us. "He's sicker than a dog on a ham. The prison doctor insisted he be taken to the hospital very late last night, and we moved him to Charing

Cross. He's gotten worse, and now he's calling for his family. I maintained my custody until I realized the man has no strength even to leave his bed. He's been complaining of terrific back pain, and the doctor took me aside to tell me his kidneys are failing. The poor man no longer has any feeling in his legs. 'You're in God's hands, now, James,' was all the doctor would say to him. Ryder wants to see his family immediately—and you, too, Holmes. I never imagined I would catch all my calves with one swing of the rope, but this will save us time. He's not long for this earth, if I am any judge. We need to hurry."

"Is Wolfgang Kern with him?"

"No, he's actually here—out in my cab. He was in Eyford when he got news of Ryder's arrest and returned with the constable who brought the message. I met him at the hospital a few hours ago. The poor chap has been wringing his hands all day over this misfortune that has befallen his partner."

"And you feel certain this man, James Ryder, is dying?"

Lestrade tightened his lip and gave an inarticulate grunt in the cynical and resigned way that men often do when they think about death. "We won't be taking the scenic route to the hospital, if that's what you mean."

"There are six of us, Lestrade. Watson and I will take the cab in which we came."

"Right, Holmes."

Lestrade hurried the two women from the house to his cab before shouting to the driver to run the horses out. Holmes jumped up on our own cab and gave some detailed instructions to the driver while flashing a coin at him. Then he swung himself down inside the carriage. The driver whipped up the horses, and we soon found ourselves gaining on Lestrade as we sped down the road at a furious pace.

Chapter Six

It would prove to be a frantic half-hour's ride to the hospital, and after Holmes sat for some moments in silence, he used the remainder of our journey to express his thoughts on the investigation.

"A fascinating study, Watson," remarked he. "I will telegram Dr. Stenerude when we return to Baker Street."

"Why not send for him upon our arrival at the hospital?" I asked.

"Can you tell me why not, Watson?"

"I suppose Lestrade's description of Ryder doesn't allow for that much time."

"My guess as well. I see that you refer to this man as 'Ryder'. I will assume you are correct and do the same, at least until the hour is past, when we shall know one way or the other if it is he. As for Stenerude, he is an esteemed London doctor who has surgeoned for over thirty years in our hospitals, and I wish to caution him about remaining in touch with Mrs. Ryder."

"Why is that?"

"Because the facts suggest that Mrs. Ryder, or possibly her daughter—we should not dismiss either possibility—has been poisoning James Ryder. Certain facts suggest this conclusion, at least.

"You're joking, Holmes! The young lady has forgiven her father. As for the mother, I heard Mrs. Ryder say some bitter things about her husband, but what could be more natural under the circumstances? I saw nothing that casts real suspicion on either one of them."

"But you are not a student of crime, Watson! The question lies in the fact that volume four of Napoleon has been read while the other three have been ignored."

"How do you know that, Holmes?"

"Because she claims to have read the first three volumes at the beginning of last summer. But Harper & Brothers has just instituted a two-letter code that encrypts the month and year of its publication on the copyright page. In the example of the Napoleonic set it translates to September of last year. So the set was published several months *after* the beginning of last summer, which was when she claims to have read the first three books. As for volume four we must ask why someone would read only one book in a set about Napoleon."

"I suppose if someone wanted to know about the end of Napoleon's career—Waterloo, and so forth—they might read just the last volume."

"That much is obvious. But if this is the case with Mrs. Ryder, it has no significance for us. No, I believe something peculiar in that last volume interested her. I have read a little about Napoleon myself, Watson. He is a fascinating character, and the end of his life is instructive to our case. It is worthwhile if we understand his background. After his capture by the British, Napoleon had hoped for exile in England while waiting below board on a British ship as it lay in dock. There he charmed the young British sailors who were delighted at having the chance to come aboard to meet the Great One. But in the end the authorities took no chances and brought him to St. Helene's, that formidable island lost in the vastness of the

Atlantic Ocean. A few years passed in relative calm, and the Emperor hoped for a transfer to the mainland. But then he began to have headaches and fevers, and gradually his legs grew weak and stiff. He grew melancholy, knowing he had once ruled armies and countries and had laid waste to entire nations, but now could hardly stand and support his own weight. His stomach, too, bore signs of sickness, and he vomited more often as the months passed. Even the doctor's recommendation that wine be taken seemed ineffective, though the Emperor's trusted servant and cook, the faithful Penard, always made sure to have a glass at his elbow.

"Well, you know the rest, Watson, if you've kept up on that monthly medical journal that has been coming to the apartment. A few scholars have pointed out that the symptoms complained of by Napoleon point to a gradual poisoning of the blood. But who would have done such a thing to the Emperor? I have found in my investigations that a man can withstand the attacks of a world around him, but rarely the betrayal of a trusted friend. So Napoleon grew worse and died, and his estate was divided up and given to his family of which a smaller portion was given to his friends. Among this latter group was Penard, who had prepared all the Master's meals. The preparation of food is an interesting one, Watson. It is said, for example, that a frog put into an open pot of boiling water will immediately jump out. But a frog put into tepid water that is slowly put to a boil will never jump out. Napoleon, so to speak, was put into a pot of tepid water by his cook. Why should the Emperor have suspected that treachery was planned against himself, since he was powerless in life? Arthur Heston pictures it well in his descriptive book on Napoleon which I read many years ago while investigating the case of the Napoleon busts. Colonel Heston envisions the dark waters of the Atlantic breaking upon the rocky edge of the island as Napoleon warms himself by the fire in his house, grandly holding forth with these, his last admirers able to appreciate his once splendid adventures. No doubt the wine flowed freely in those nostalgic days, as the talk of old campaigns and expeditions added their own warmth to the log-stoked hearth that battled the damp winter nights. But all the while death lay at his elbow. Napoleon had often despised it while fighting opposing armies in forests, fields, and glens while hundreds of miles from France, and scorned its presence in salty marshes and boggy mires bloodstained with his soldiers' blood. But now it would claim him across the absurd space of six inches of tablecloth while hidden inside Trojan gifts—bottles tainted with tiny amounts of poison, probably arsenic, dissolved in the Emperor's favorite wine and poured into his glass. There the poison waited patiently for the end of a narrative or the close of a joke, when it would be consumed, causing no more immediate effect than would a small group of soldiers in a single foray of a much larger war. But in the end, the slow accumulation of skirmishes can topple a mighty foe. And so it happened with Napoleon. Confident he was adored by those around him, he never suspected that a war was being waged against his life, or that his personal cook would succeed where nations and armies had failed.

"Now we come to the present and see that James Ryder has complained of all the symptoms known to Napoleon. He has headaches and fever, weakness and stiffness of the legs, nausea and stomach pain. We know, too, that wine has been a constant staple in his diet. Do we suppose these symptoms and happenings are mere coincidences? We will examine the bottles to be sure, but I believe this man is dying an unnatural death—death by poison! There is murder at hand, Watson, whether this man be Ryder or not. I believe we will certainly need to look more closely into the activities of Wolfgang Kern."

"You suspect him?"

"His access to Ryder and to the wine bottles makes him a natural suspect, not to mention his love of money and ambitious nature. Whoa, there, Watson! Brace yourself."

I had been thrown upon the door as the driver turned the carriage sharply round a corner.

Holmes gave a wry smile. "It won't do to startle some pedestrian by having a gentleman fly across his path," said he.

"I don't think we are following Lestrade anymore," I replied.

"No, we're taking a shorter route. The ride is a bit rougher, but we should get to the hospital sooner than Lestrade. I wish to see Ryder before they arrive, if at all possible."

"You suspect he was poisoned by Kern or one of the Ryder women?"

"Mrs. Ryder is certainly hiding something, but whether she is acting alone is uncertain. After all, her daughter, Rachel, would have just as many reasons to hate her father. She may still secretly blame him for her brother's death and for her mother's inconsolable spirit. She has already admitted to smashing her father's violin in anger. Can we be sure she handles her emotions differently now, simply because she is older? Who can know what smoldering fires might lay in the bosom of a young woman whose brother and mother were cruelly wronged?"

"It still surprises me, Holmes, that you gave no indication last night while talking with Miss Ryder that she was a suspect."

"But we must follow the facts wherever they lead us. We cannot simply dismiss her on the basis of her gender or age. In a way I believe I told her as much."

"I think she is innocent," I replied.

"And you are often right regarding the fair sex, Watson. Still, consider the following possibility; had Rachel Ryder wanted to kill her father she might feign friendliness toward him in order to gain his trust. She might even form a secret tryst with Kern in order to have access to the wine bottles, either directly or indirectly. Indeed, how can we exclude the possibility that both Ryder women have worked in concert with each other, or with Kern, for that matter?"

"But if Rachel Ryder were trying to kill her father why would she bother coming to our apartment?"

"She would have come in response to my letter to find out how much I knew."

"No, Holmes, don't you remember? She said she never got your communiqué. You yourself said that her arrival was a coincidence."

"And so I thought at the time. But listen to yourself, Watson. She *said* she did not get my communiqué. We only have her word for that."

"Well, regardless, Holmes, I think I will maintain her innocence."

"Time will tell, Doctor," said he as he bit down hard on his pipe. I had learned over the years that Holmes rarely called me 'Doctor' unless he entertained some inward private doubt about a particular point in a case where we fell opposite each other. I made a mental note of his comment but maintained my faith in the young woman.

"And what, Holmes," I inquired, "is your further impression of Kern? Lestrade claims he has been wringing his hands all day over his partner's condition."

"Yes. And I couldn't help but notice that Mrs. Ryder was also upset."

"But their reactions seem to go against your suspicions of them. If either of them was trying to kill him, why would he or she be upset that Ryder was sick?"

"Facts are curious things, Watson. Two persons can look at the same effects without seeing their causes, and come up with different, even contradictory explanations. It makes for many of the lively arguments in the world. I agree with you that Mrs. Ryder was genuinely upset to hear that this man who calls himself 'Ryder' was in the hospital. But it does not necessarily mean she can be dismissed as a suspect. But here is Charing Cross, Watson, and I believe our driver has earned the sovereign I promised him; Lestrade is no where in sight."

Holmes tipped the driver and hurried past the front columns of the hospital and gave forth his most commanding air to an old watchman at the desk.

"Right, Mr. Holmes," said the grizzled man who appeared to recognize my companion, and we followed this stooped figure along several corridors into the heart of the building. As we progressed I became aware of an increase in odor, and I held my hand over my nose, for despite being a doctor I never fully reconciled myself to the combined strength of chloroform and ammonia found most potent in a hospital. We followed the man around the corner of a corridor and down some steps until we reached a room from which a low moaning could be heard. We entered the sick room and found a young red-haired orderly standing by the bed on which a ghastly pale figure of a man lay dying.

"Watson!" cried Holmes in a whisper, waving and pointing his hand in an effort to get me to examine the man. I stepped forward and felt his wrist and forehead. The man's pulse was weak and his skin clammy and moist. I noticed his fevered brow and than looked carefully at the rest of his face. Though time had worn its lines into the once-youthful face of James Ryder I immediately knew from our past acquaintance that this man was certainly he. I looked at Holmes whose eyes, too, had settled on the man, and seeming to read my very thought he nodded in agreement. Ryder continued to moan softly in a semi-conscious state, and his respiration was low and erratic.

"Who goes there?" cried a loud voice behind us.

We turned and saw a distinguished looking gentleman enter the room with a stethoscope about his neck, and with a bottle in one hand and a hypodermic syringe in the other. "What are you doing here? he demanded. "Stand back!" Holmes rose slowly as though in abject humbleness, then sprang with both hands against the man's chest and shoved the doctor out of the room. Managing to stay just inside the threshold Holmes then locked the door. The man yelled at Holmes with an oath and cried for the watchman to come with his keys. He pounded the door with his fists and railed against Holmes in terrible threatening screams. My friend went into a state of immediate concentration however, and leaned over Ryder and looked at him expectantly. Then, for an instant, the flow of Death itself receded as a tiny ebbing wave on the shore of eternity, and James Ryder bestirred his body as it awakened to the shouting noises about him. He opened his eyes and fixed them on Holmes. A faint smile then came to his face, evident more in his eyes than in any upturn of the mouth, and his lips parted slowly as the recognition of my companion now moistened his eyes for the last time. Holmes bent over and whispered something in his ear. With extraordinary effort Ryder lifted his head off the pillow and made a last effort to speak. The orderly and I followed Holmes in leaning over the bed to hear the last words of the dying man. They failed, being hardly audible, yet by the movement of his lips we were able to read his last wish as his body sank down and expired upon the bed.

A moment passed as I checked for signs of life. "He's gone, Holmes," said I.

Holmes raised his figure in slow deliberation until his whole body and head were erect; then he raised his chin even more, and I saw upon his hawk-like features an effort at thought, or of dignity, or of an attempt to pierce some veil of mystery that hung upon this moment.

"Holmes! Holmes!" a voice cried out. "Open the door! It is I, Lestrade!"

My friend lowered his head with a sigh and the transfixed moment was gone. "Open the door, will you, Watson?" he asked.

I did as he bid, and in came Lestrade, Wolfgang Kern, Rachel and Elisabeth Ryder, and, of course, the hospital doctor, who was still beside himself with rage. Miss Ryder saw her father dead upon the bed and gave a cry as she broke into convulsive weeping.

"Arrest this man, inspector!" cried the doctor.

"Mr. Holmes, I must ask you to leave," said Lestrade with enough feigned sense of authority to satisfy the doctor, but with reluctance in his voice.

I followed Holmes and Lestrade to outside the building where Lestrade looked at my companion and scratched his head. "I'll be the first to admit I seldom understand your methods, Holmes. But the doctor has a point. What was the idea of shoving him out of the room and locking the door?"

"I hoped for an altercation."

"You certainly got that."

"It was a long shot to hope the doctor's noise would break through the fog of Ryder's mind and give us a last moment with him, but there were no alternatives."

"Did it work?"

"He mouthed a few words about forgetting. Then he died."

"That's not very helpful. I was hoping he would have remembered something. I had hoped he would tell us who he thought poisoned him."

"You believe Ryder was poisoned?"

"I didn't wish to say anything in front of the others, Holmes, but yes, the doctor believes he was poisoned. I must find out if the poisoning was accidental or not. I will take the rail to Ryder's house to-morrow afternoon to see if I can find some evidence. I have already charged the constable to allow you into the villa should you wish to make your own investigation."

"That's good of you, Lestrade."

"I'm good in the bargain, Holmes. I've not forgotten what you did for me in the Frankl case. You're off then?"

"Yes, and thank you for the opportunity. I will take the first train tomorrow. In the meantime it is essential that Kern does not return to Ryder's house, for even the accidental tampering of evidence could prove disastrous."

"I'll see to it, Holmes."

"By the way, did Wolfgang Kern talk very much with either of the Ryder women on the way to the hospital?"

"Not at all. From the moment I arrived at Mrs. Ryder's house he said he had a bad chill, and he practically covered his face with a muffler. He was still that way at the hospital, if you noticed. He may be sick, but he'll be talking soon enough when I ask him about the habits of James Ryder. Poisoning a man is serious business, and I aim to find out who did it, if that is what happened. Kern was a member of the household, you know."

"Yes. Well, good luck, then, Lestrade! One other thing. I won't be assisting you for some time. Watson and I are leaving for America to-morrow afternoon."

"What? America? That doesn't sound like you, Holmes."

"My publisher in the States wants me to promote my new book on philosophy. We'll be traveling to various cities beginning at New York."

"Taking that new skiff over there, are you?"

"Yes," said Holmes with slight bemusement at the incongruent analogy. "I guess you could call it that."

"Well, *bon voyage*, then."

Chapter Seven

Deciding that our schedule on the morrow would leave us little time for errands when we returned from Eyford, Holmes and I spent the evening packing our clothes for our trip across the Atlantic. We finished late in the evening, and though it had been an exhausting day I still found sleeping impossible. The pathos of Ryder dying, the suspicions surrounding the Ryder women and Wolfgang Kern, and the anticipations of our trip to Ryder's house followed by the commencement of our ocean voyage caused too much excitement for my nerves. Not until I noticed the first light of morning did I finally drop off to sleep, and I had not been resting for more than an hour when a voice roused me from slumber.

"Watson, are you coming?"

I opened my eyes and saw Holmes already dressed. "I allowed you to sleep as long as I could, Watson, but if you wish to catch the train to Eyford we have but a few moments."

Without a word I struggled into my clothes and grabbed a biscuit on my way out of the house, practically stumbling upon the curb and into the carriage where Holmes was already waiting.

"Excellent!" cried Holmes as he wrapped the head of his cane on the roof of the carriage. "There are a few points of evidence worth checking at the Ryder house. I won't be surprised if some of the evidence is missing, but it is worth the attempt."

It was an hour-and-a-half later by rail and by cart when we found ourselves at the front door of Ryder's house. The constable recognized the name on Holmes's card, and we entered the double arched oaken doors of the villa. Holmes wasted no time and went immediately to the kitchen where he found an open bottle of wine. He carefully poured out the remaining liquid and collected its dregs onto a flat dish. Then Holmes took out his magnifying glass to look at the debris more closely, and I heard him give a cry of delight "I suspected as much," said he. "Our trip has already been justified, Watson. Let us have a look below." I followed Holmes down some narrow winding steps that led to the dirt floor of the cellar, and there we found a wine rack in which about two-dozen bottles were stored. My companion lit a candle he had brought with him and began to examine the top surface of all the corks with his magnifier. He had passed several bottles until his attention riveted upon one in particular, and he gave a grunt of satisfaction. "Look here, Watson," he exclaimed, inviting me to peer into the glass. "What do you make of that?"

I looked and saw a speck of blue no bigger than a few grains of sand. "Do you mean this tiny speck here?" I asked.

"Yes, that is it. I am pleased to find it here, though I suspected its presence before we ever arrived. We will leave it for Lestrade. I doubt this speck is large enough to be tested for its age, but I believe we may draw an inference from it, nonetheless. The Director of the Louvre is no longer a suspect in the death of Ryder."

"The Director? I didn't even know he was under suspicion."

"Most certainly he was—to me, at least—but this clears him of any murder. Just grab any of these other bottles, Watson. They are all poisoned, but less Lestrade miss the entire *modus operandi* and Kern then destroy the bottles, I want Lestrade to have some circumstantial evidence against the murderers."

"Murderers, Holmes? Who are they?"

"There are two, Watson."

I was about to ask him which two these were, but some edge in his voice told me my question would be better asked on a later occasion. There was always in Holmes a love to sequester for himself certain knowledge for an indefinite period of time. It was part of his identity, and, if I may be less flattering about him for a moment, was the primary way I believe he achieved a sense of power. These moments were that for which he played the game, and even I, his closet friend, was not allowed into that sanctum of knowledge before he was ready.

We left the Ryder house and boarded our train for London, and during the return journey Holmes wrote a note to Lestrade telling him the New York address where he would be staying. By noon we were back at Baker Street to gather our things for our ocean trip. Holmes had posted the letter, and we were about to leave with bags in hand when we heard the closing of the outside door followed by the sound of someone talking with Mrs. Hudson in the passageway. Then there came a firm tread upon the stair and a distinct knock on the door. Holmes and I looked at one another with puzzled expressions, for we were not expecting visitors.

"Come in!" cried Holmes.

The door opened and there stepped into our room Mr. Wolfgang Kern, who announced his own name, and said he was the leading promoter of dubious art. I saw quickly that this man, despite whatever villainy he represented, had that natural charm about him which not only women, but even men admired. It was a manner born of a natural, easy charisma and punctuated by a handsome appearance. He was tall, flawless in his dress, and clean-shaven upon his tightly chiseled features. He was also athletic in build, swarthy in complexion,

Kern had a natrual, easy charisma about him.

and debonair enough to carry off a convincing braggadocio in even small matters, as in the way he smoked.

"I needed to see you before I left for America, Mr. Holmes," said he, drawing deeply upon a cigarette.

"Perhaps that has saved me the trouble of looking you up at a much later date," replied my companion. "Please take a seat."

"Oh, you wanted to see me about something?"

"We'll come to that later. What brings you here?"

"I understand from the newspapers that you are about to embark on a speaking tour in the United States, and that you and your friend have two tickets for a transatlantic crossing."

"Oh, but our small entourage is full. I'm afraid you won't be traveling together with Dr. Watson and me."

Kern smiled and looked fixedly at my companion. "I fully realize that. You see, I hope to take your tickets from you and use them for myself and for my new partner, Mr. Greeley. The paintings are already crated and waiting for us on the dock. We're traveling over to the biggest American cities to show Ryder's work and to build up enthusiasm for it. The Armory Show is only a year away and, speaking frankly, Holmes, as one *charlatan* to another, I hope to generate interest in the paintings and boost their value considerably. America is so impressionable, you know. A lawyer, Mr. Greeley, bought out Ryder's share of ownership in the paintings a few days before Ryder was arrested. He now wants to oversee his investment personally, and hence our need for two tickets to cross the Atlantic. We prefer not to pay for these ourselves, and besides, I'm a little short of money."

"Just a penny or two?" asked Holmes, coolly. "I understand there are still a few left on James Ryder's eyes."

"Very funny, Mr. Holmes. If you have something to say to me, then say it."

"In due course," replied my friend. "As for the tickets, they are only second class."

"Second class on this ship is better than first class on most others. They'll be good enough."

"Excuse me, Kern," I said with some heat, "but not many a man would lack the etiquette to call a gentleman a 'charlatan' in that gentleman's own apartments. Might I inquire about your forwardness?"

"Wonderful, Doctor!" remarked Kern in genuine admiration. "I love how that last complaint rippled so gracefully off your tongue. It's the same with your writing. You are irreplaceable in the trio."

"The trio?"

"You don't have to act naïve, Doctor. Acting is Holmes's job, not yours or Lestrade's."

"It appears," said Holmes wearily to me, "that Mr. Kern has some theory he wants to advance to us, Watson."

"Aye! I do!" said Kern with a wink. "I want you both to know that I see past all of your artifices."

"Really?" replied Holmes. "I am delighted to hear it. Please tell us more."

"There's a lot of empty time to fill on an island," said Kern, looking hard at Holmes, "and I learned years ago from Jimmy Ryder that reading can keep a man sane. So I have read many books on all kinds of subjects. None of these interested me, however, as much as Dr. Watson's stories about his friend, Sherlock Holmes. Of course, I never believed for a minute that an amateur could do all the things attributed to Holmes. Only a Scotland Yard detective working with other Yarders could affect the kind of results that Watson wrote about. But the character of Holmes was brilliant. In fact, I found in him my own inspiration to become a promoter."

"I believe your comment about the Yarders is the greatest compliment ever given me," remarked Holmes.

"As for Lestrade," continued Kern, holding up a hand for silence, "I never met a more dull fellow in my life. He has the personality of a tomato. Yet how people underestimate him!

For genius lay in this man, Lestrade, to think of such a scheme—a scheme to tell the world of the exploits of one, Sherlock Holmes. And so he found a writer—you, Dr. Watson, and then an actor—you, Mr. Holmes, to do the two things he *could not*. In the course of his many investigations Lestrade would naturally come across many crimes, some more colourful than others. Here and there a good story could be had with a little imaginative storytelling. All he needed was a good creative writer and then someone who would be more mercurial than himself to be the *prima donna* in these tales— an eccentric actor able to capture the public's imagination. The stories could be sold to magazines, and if such Holmes stories became popular, a lot of money could be made. He would split the proceeds three ways, and this arrangement with you two could continue for a long time. Of course, he would appear now and again in these narratives, always being the dolt in the story. He would eat crow and look stupid, but even duping the public in self-effacement could be amusing if one maintained a sense of humor." Kern finished with an emphasized flourish of the hand.

Holmes sat up in his chair with a hopeful look. "He's on to us, Watson," said he. "Do you suppose, Kern, that if your theory were published among a sympathetic public that Dr. Watson would have to discontinue these romanticized stories about me?"

"Most undoubtedly, Holmes."

"Remarkable! Really quite remarkable! The stories are, as you suggest, shamelessly fanciful."

"I was coming to just that point," replied Kern as he adopted a lecturing tone. "I first began to suspect the fanciful elements in Dr. Watson's stories when I read about John Drebber the Utah Mormon in *A Study In Scarlet*."

"Ah, yes, that was my first case with Dr. Watson quite some time ago. I don't recall all the details."

"I'm not surprised, Holmes, since you were merely coached by Lestrade, and were obviously not a real player in the drama."

"Perhaps you can refresh my memory."

"I was counting on it," said Kern with a frozen smile. "In fact, the plan of John Drebber's enemy, the wronged Jefferson Hope, bears directly on how I will obtain your two tickets, as well as discourage Lestrade's prosecution of me in the Ryder case. The matter is simple, really. We need only remember the facts of so many years ago regarding this man, Hope."

"Pray continue," said Holmes.

"You might recall that Hope's kidnapped fiancé died from a broken heart after being forced into marriage with this scoundrel, Drebber. Years later Hope cornered Drebber with two indistinguishable pills: one poison, the other harmless. Jefferson Hope did not want to be the direct agent of Drebber's death, but he believed there was a Providence, and that if Drebber were given a choice between the two pills he would pick the poisoned one. Drebber, of course, picked the poison. And whose testimony do we have for all these fanciful events told us in *A Study In Scarlet*, including the overdone western evocation of American wilderness? Why, it is Dr. Watson, recording the doings of that wondrous trio—Sherlock Holmes, Lestrade, and himself!"

Kern's sarcasm was maddening, but Holmes held his peace.

"I know what you gentlemen are thinking," added Kern. 'He has no real evidence against our trio. He cannot prove it.' And you are right. The newspapers would denounce my insight as mere speculation, as just another attempt by Kern the Promoter to grab more headlines. No, I could never prove it to *them*. But I will prove it to both of *you* in my presence." As he spoke Kern drew from inside his jacket pocket a small leather pouch with a drawstring and a flap. He opened it and turned the pouch upside down on the table before him. Slowly he lifted it to reveal two small marbles, one black and one white. "These are from my father's Freemason days," he remarked. Again he reached into his coat, and this time pulled out a group of folded papers which he straightened on his knee in a manner not unlike a shoe-shiner's cloth upon a shoe. He held them up. Holmes and I read in bold letters across the top of the first page: A STUDY WITHOUT SCARLET: or, What Wolfgang Kern Had To Tell.

"I know that Lestrade has talked to the doctor at the hospital, and that I am a possible suspect in Ryder's death," said Kern, matter-of-factly. "This here is my bloodless, albeit detailed, confession of how I poisoned James Ryder. I have not signed it, however. After all, there is not really enough evidence for a sure conviction. I know you will admit, Holmes, if you have any brains at all, that Lestrade's evidence is merely circumstantial against me. I had a hypodermic syringe in my possession and access to the wine bottles. Besides these facts is only Lestrade's very speculative motive that I wanted to kill Ryder before he sold his paintings too prematurely."

"Perhaps," said Holmes, "Lestrade could add that you and the embittered Mrs. Ryder are brother and sister."

Kern sat up with a start. "So you know about that, Holmes. How did you find out?"

"I had a reliable source."

"Lestrade, of course!" cried Kern, laughing. "Ever the actor, aren't we, Mr. Holmes. I suppose that Lestrade is sharpening his knives, preparing for some clever barrister to carve me up in front of a jury by pouncing upon my temporary possession of the Director's hypodermic, and supposing I was used it at my sister's request. No doubt this barrister can also open one of the poisoned wine bottles before the very eyes of the jurists and pour out its damning evidence. 'There!' I hear him cry in hysteria as a solemn hush falls upon the courtroom. '*There* is the diameter of corkstrand that fits the hollow of Kern's syringe!' What verdict do ye return?'

"Pardon the interruption," said Holmes, "but such a dramatic scene is unlikely. The corkstrand will need to dry overnight to be shown that it came from your syringe. The strand will have been soaked and expanded due to its immersion in the wine."

For a moment Kern was taken aback at Holmes's insight, but then a bitter smile returned to his face. "The Yarders really tell you everything, don't they? So confess, Holmes, the evidence is incomplete at best, and speculative at worst. I would say the odds are about even as to whether a jury would convict me."

"I agree," said Holmes.

"Then look upon my coming as a stroke of luck. You can serve me up to Lestrade on a silver platter if only the lot goes against me. I am offering you an even chance of a sure prosecution. If I pick the black marble I will sign this confession. If I pick the white marble I gain two costly tickets to steam across the ocean and the even greater satisfaction of having proved in my presence that both of you are imposters."

I cast a skeptical glance at Holmes. "How," I asked Kern, "do we know you will keep your end of the bargain?"

"You and Holmes have my most solemn oath upon the grave of my dead nephew," he replied. "He was small when he died, but he took the greater part of my sister's heart with him. I have my brother-in-law to thank for that. I've no wife, and little Barney was the closest thing to a son I ever had."

"You were away in Ceylon and never met him," replied Holmes as he rolled the marbles between his fingers. Holmes thought long upon the matter. "As for drawing a lot," he said, "I believe that justice isn't that simple. I don't ever recall any system of law that picked a certain coloured marble to see if it coincided with the guilt or innocence of accused persons when evidence was known. Had such a system proven itself, the need for judges and juries would never have arisen. I cannot agree that throwing dice, for example, would have saved everyone a lot of time and trouble in trying criminal cases. However, I agree to a parley in this instance. The evidence is, as you say, circumstantial, and you would deny in court that you had ever made this verbal confession to Dr. Watson and me. I would also prefer a signed confession because international prosecution is often unsuccessful. What do you think, Watson?"

"I would not hesitate, Holmes," I said, with a wave of my fist. "Take up the gauntlet! We may be sure he will run foul in a lot; let us remember Hope and Drebber!"

"Very well. I will first inspect the marbles. Any objections, Kern?"

"Definitely not," replied he. "And the Doctor's ticket?"

"I will reimburse Watson if—"

"That will not be necessary, Holmes," I replied. "It will be worth my while to see Kern get his comeuppance. If there is a God in heaven, Kern will pick the black marble."

"A black marble for the blackguard, eh, Doctor?" queried Kern with a smile.

Holmes shook his head at Kern's pathetic arrogance and picked up the marbles and placed them on a small weighing scale. He then lifted them off with measuring calipers and observed them minutely with his magnifying glass. Satisfied, he held each one up to a magnet. Finally, he laid them both upon a playing card that spanned a tall water-filled glass. He snapped his middle finger sideways so that the card flew off the cup's rim, and the two marbles fell evenly to the bottom. Holmes emptied the glass, dried the marbles, and placed the two spheres back into the pouch and pulled the drawstring. Then he shook it vigorously. Folding over the flap of the pouch he laid the little leather bag flat upon the table so that the opening faced himself and so that the pouch lay halfway between he and Kern. The hidden marbles protruded beneath the leather skin.

"Which shall it be?" said Holmes to Kern. "Point. And do not touch."

With a weary smile Kern unfolded his hands upon his chest so that one of his wrists and fingers could rotate outward and point to the little leather bag. "My life, my way, *my right!*" said he.

Holmes reached down, and, keeping the protruding marbles in plain view of us all, unfolded the bag's mouth and turned the pouch around to face Kern. With a careful motion he took his thumb and put pressure upon the leather skin so that the chosen marble slid toward the opening of the bag. Even now, as I think upon this scene of several years ago, I do not think I can convey to my readers that terrible thrill and the absolute dumbstruck vexation that coursed through me when I saw the Italian carerra surface of the tiny white marble emerge from its leathery cover. It seemed that in a single moment all the forces of darkness had exalted themselves.

A smug look of triumph strode boldly across Kern's face. He picked up the two tickets and the unsigned confessional from the table and placed them jauntily into his pocket. "You may keep the bag of marbles for yourself, Holmes, as a souvenir of this meeting. You can store them in that trunk of memorabilia Watson is always driveling about. I'm sure they'll stay there. I doubt that Dr. Watson will want this one for the Holmes annals."

Holmes nodded, trying to take in the full import of having lost the lot, and muttering as much to himself as to us that "one less of Watson's stories seems to be the only silver lining to this cloud."

"Well, I'm off," said Kern, rising. "Our ship leaves in a few hours and I must tell Greeley the good news. For the record Mr. Holmes, I would have been greatly distressed had I picked the black marble."

"No doubt you would have," replied my friend.

"Oh, less for myself than for my sister. The poor creature has suffered enough in this life. I wouldn't want her to know her brother was a murderer, or see me tried before the courts. It's best that she thinks her husband died of natural causes."

"Oh, you needn't worry about your sister thinking *that*," replied Holmes.

"Oh? Why is that? Are you going to tell her about me?"

For an answer Holmes handed Ryder his magnifier and reached for the poisoned bottle. "Just take a closer look, here, Kern, while I turn this bottle upside down. Tell me what you see floating along the top."

I heard a sharp intake of breath as Kern peered through the glass, and in one instant all his arrogance left him. His face fell, and he let out a groan.

"The *two* corkstrands are visible without the glass," said Holmes, "but I wanted to give you a better look."

I saw a variety of emotions pass over Kern as he struggled with this new information. Finally a light grew in his eye. "So now you know I returned to the cellar to double the poison in the bottle, Holmes."

"With what?—the hypodermic you borrowed from the Director?"

"Of course, what else?"

"Look again with the glass, Kern. Note in particular how one strand is slightly thicker than the other."

Kern bent over the bottle again to observe the strands of cork that floated upon the surface of the wine like two dark snakes in a murky pond. Again he uttered a groan in vexation and slowly laid down the magnifier.

"Two different strands, Kern," stated my friend, "and so two different murderers. You never suspected your sister was capable of such an act, did you? You can live with that knowledge now. I'm sure when we show her the two strands she will be just as shocked about you. She might, however, still try and protect you by assuming the entire guilt in the affair. Perhaps that genius you admire, Lestrade, will pour out the wine and examine the pieces of cork more closely after they have dried. If so, I assure you that he is unlikely to see the minute difference between them. He, too, will join your sister in stating that she alone is the murderer. If you leave for America now, your sister's guilt will go unshared, and her punishment be greater."

Kern seemed irresolute for a moment, but then his features set still and hard. "You want me to sign my confession, don't you, Holmes? Well, your evidence against my sister is not convincing. In fact, I don't see any evidence. How did she poison the bottles, for example?"

"She had a syringe," replied my companion, picking from the shelf a large Bible and laying it down upon the table between he and Kern. He opened the gilded engraved front cover and lifted out a small wooden case that lay in a hollow that had been cut out of the text block. Then he closed the cover, and the outer edges of the Bible looked as normal as any other book. "I took the family Bible from her bookcase," said Holmes. "She probably hadn't thought about the syringe being inside it for years. This wooden case and hypodermic were given to your father as a gift upon his graduation from veterinarian studies at the university he attended. These special sized syringes are only made by Fenner & du Bois. As a veterinarian your father needed the needle to treat all kinds of animals, including large ones. The veterinarian's needle is slightly larger and longer than those used upon people. Years later your father retired, and sometime afterward you found a different use for it when you became addicted to cocaine."

"That's a stinking lie, Holmes!" said Kern, pointing a cigarette at my companion.

"You preferred a solution of five percent, Kern, if my memory serves me right from my days at the Bar Of Gold. You should remember from reading Watson's stories that I occasionally visited that opium den in my investigations. I believe you called yourself 'Walter' then. And correct me if I'm wrong, but the folks at the Bar of Gold were not the only ones who knew of your addiction. Your sister also found out and became alarmed. She knew the habit was destructible and doubtless thought the syringe should be thrown away. But she may have also regarded it as a family keepsake, a memento of her father—the one whom she doubly loved for his having come to her rescue when her husband deserted her. So she hid the needle to keep you from finding it, assuming, as she did, that you would throw the house into a shambles when the temptation for the drug seized you. I suppose she then lied about throwing it out, hoping it would stop you from looking for it. Instead she hid it inside this large family Bible—in the one place she believed a cocaine addict would not look. The outer brass latch might even stay closed during a ransacking of the library."

"My sister would never deface such a book. You're lying about that, too. Just a walking theatre, aren't you, Holmes—actor, playwright, and stage all rolled into one."

"You're entitled to your opinion, Kern. But you have been away in Ceylon too long to know the full depths of despair gripping your sister. I, for one, believe she cut out the Bible text with few qualms. Virtually any woman would grow cold in her religious faith if her husband deserted her and her son died. In that moment of trying to hide the syringe I don't doubt that she valued the old family Bible more for the practical solution it could give in that instant, than for its spiritual and idealistic concepts that once succored her. Her daughter, Rachel Anne, found a stack of Bible pages thrown out with some rotted firewood shortly before you deserted her and her mother. There was nothing besides these things, not even the book cover. When asked, Miss Ryder also remembered nothing shining back at her from the Bible text as she examined it, though she implied that the weather was clear and the moon full. Yet most Bibles of this age have their foredging gilded, and full pages should have reflected their edging in the moonlight as she turned them over. I deduced that the Bible's cover and the outer edging of the text-block had therefore been preserved. What else besides a hiding place within the Bible could account for these changes? The pleasure of deducing this fact amused me at the time, though later I saw with concern its probable connection to the illness of James Ryder. No, Kern—enough picking of marbles for one day. Your sister, not you, is under Lestrade's scope of suspicion. He is detaining her—" Holmes glanced at the mantle clock, "*right now*— as we speak. I can do nothing for her. Once confronted with his questions I believe she will have to give answers."

"You have *all* the answers, don't you, Holmes?" said Kern, with a sneer.

"I fancy I have at least one or two. The fact that you and she were *both* involved in his murder clears up one little mystery, however. You both reacted with genuine surprise when you heard that Ryder was taken to the hospital, and for a while I wondered if I were on the wrong track altogether. But after examining the corkstrands more closely I noticed there was a difference in their thickness, and therefore the strands must have come from different syringes. Had you doubled the poison you would doubtless have used the same syringe. Because there were two syringes used, there were two murderers. Then another thought struck me. What if two people had poisoned the bottles *without knowing what the other did?* That would explain your reactions perfectly, for you were both surprised when Ryder suddenly became sick, knowing the poison should have been working more slowly. Criminals who act together sometimes turn upon the other, but in your case the solitary decisions of you and your sister to poison the bottles alone led to your undoings. Probably each of you did not want the other to know that he or she had lost their integrity so far as to commit murder. As a result, the poison was doubled, and the affect upon Ryder was greater than either of you intended. His symptoms intensified to a point where they could no longer be disguised as a gradual onset of some mystery illness, a fact that potentially exposed your deed, and naturally caused you great worry. And not without warrant, for Ryder's condition has aroused suspicion at the hospital, and the doctor is now convinced Ryder has been poisoned."

Kern looked harried, and without warning he sprang from his chair. His answer was as brief and abrupt as it was unexpected. "I don't believe the evidence against my sister will hold up, Mr. Holmes. At any rate, I'm not prepared to give up my freedom on a bluff from you. Any testimony from me will only be misunderstood and create further suspicion on both Elisabeth and me. No, it's best if I just leave on the ship. Elisabeth will understand the situation and know how to handle herself. She's always been good at that. *Au revoir*, then," said he, as he stepped from the room, and the last glimpse we would ever have of Wolfgang Kern was the bare teeth of his insufferable smile as he turned his head back in defiance as he descended the stair.

"The ways of Divinity are inscrutable, Watson," said Holmes, when our visitor had left. "This man, Kern, is as bad a fellow as we have had occasion to meet, and yet he picks the one marble that gives him the freedom of flight. At least he showed his full hand to us before he left. He was unwilling to share his sister's fate if she were prosecuted. 'I'll have my freedom, sir!' says he, and 'Elisabeth can handle herself.' What kind of man speaks that way, Watson?"

"I agree. He is the worst of characters. And yet, Holmes, he did try to blame himself for the doubling of the poison."

"Yes, but there was no bravery there. Kern knew if we believed his story about him being the only murderer, the white marble he picked would still pledge him our immunity. Once we showed him other evidence against his sister he responded cowardly. How ironic that he has taken the same path as that chosen by his brother-in-law thirteen years ago, who put his selfish interests before his family. In claiming to murder his brother-in-law for desertion he is his own condemnation. He unwittingly shows what punishment he thinks his own act is deserving of. But we, too, are the losers, Watson. Kern will now take Ryder's paintings across the ocean and probably make a lot of money from his foul deed. Perhaps I made a mistake in giving him an opportunity to flee, but I was compelled by the recent and disturbing trend in court cases; a number of defendants have been acquitted where the evidence against them has been purely circumstantial."

"I think Kern's cowardice shows he wouldn't have signed the confession in any event, Holmes. I believe he came on the chance to insult us, and to try to prove his absurd theory about Lestrade."

"Your explanation has the charm of consistency, Watson, though we cannot be sure exactly what Kern would have done. We know, at least, that he has abandoned his sister to her guilt." For a moment Holmes fell silent as he riffled the closed edging of the Bible with his thumb while he picked up a newspaper with his other hand. "Well, Watson," said he with a resigned and bitter smile, "we can hardly expect that all men will get a just recompense in this life. In fact, very few of them do."

I could tell from his clouded brow, however, that Holmes was hardly comforted in this knowledge, or with the lot chosen earlier by a cavalier Kern. His thoughts must have continued in this vein for some time, for the *Globe* lay in his lap for an hour before he ever turned a page of it.

Chapter Eight

During the next several days Holmes rarely left the apartment, choosing instead to fidget about the room in nervous agitation, lost in thought, and consuming more cigars than I can ever remember. "Ryder's money, Watson! Where is it?" replied he, when I asked upon what he was expending such energy of thought. During this time he read and re-read the paper, hardly ate, stayed in his bathrobe all day, drolled on his violin at unexpected hours, and took turns either pacing the floor or lounging from one seat or sofa to another. Now and then, this included a place on the divan, where, for whole mornings or evenings, he closed his eyes and remained so still that I never knew if he was transporting himself to some higher plane of analytical deduction, or simply falling to sleep. A few afternoons he went out, but was never gone for more than several hours. Finally on the Monday following Kern's departure I ventured to ask Holmes, who had apparently stayed up much of the previous night sustaining himself with something he called 'tithe tea' (his own concoction of mixed teas boiled down to a tenth of their original volume), if he wished to take a walk around the Strand. I promised him the air there had a reported visibility of more than eighteen inches. "I suppose it *is* a bit thick in here," said he, chagrined, as he batted the heavy blue air in front of his face.

We left the dense atmosphere of poisonous tobacco behind us and within a half-an-hour found ourselves strolling about the park, and observing the various buds and blooms that showed all the beginning signs of spring. The day was beautiful and the place was full with people. Though one might think that Holmes would find such a place repulsive to his natural desire for anonymity, such was not the case. Short of being alone in his apartment at Baker Street where he loved the thought of being surrounded by some millions of people swarming about, all who, by their sheer volume in number, he knew would provide him opportunities for criminal investigation, he loved to visit the park and mutter aloud his thoughts in running dialogue whenever we passed someone on the walk. Today was no different.

"A governess with her Mistress's children," he observed as we passed a young woman with children about her. "Employed sometime after fall, but not far into winter; one child is sick and not with her. What have we here? A housepainter who has just come from a postcard vendor and an antiques shop—but not very happy with the owner of the latter. No mystery in these two; a couple who has recently celebrated a wedding anniversary, their twenty-fifth unless I am much mistaken. The woman knits in her spare time and has recently burned the top of her hand while baking at the oven. The man is a barrister and politician. A closer look at that thermometer tiepin would certainly prove interesting. And halloa! What is this? A young man whose pet monkey at home has the habit of pulling his owner's left earlobe whenever he is hungry for potatoes and peas, and pulling his owner's right one when he wishes for veal and carrots." Holmes looked over at me to see if I was following him, and I nodded in return. My companion let out a murmured laugh. "No, Watson," said he, "just joking about that last one." Holmes continued to faintly smile at each person as they passed, and they returned the gesture, hardly knowing that my companion's grin was not conceived from any feeling of friendship formed from a grand sense of the brotherhood of man, but rather for their having provided him an hour of amusement in the science of observation and deduction. I sometimes thought, however, that in one respect they should have faired better at Holmes's hands than to have appeared to him as little more than so many propositions in a Euclidean problem; for their presence did, in fact, divert him from that deep-set melancholia of his betimes ragged and depressed life.

After a while Holmes relaxed his stride, and I commented to him in an offhand way that I hoped he was making progress in finding Ryder's money. To my surprise he began to talk freely of it, and I congratulated myself silently for suggesting the change in our surroundings that had apparently helped Holmes overcome his stagnant ruminations in the apartment.

"There are still some unresolved points about the Ryder case," said Holmes, as we continued our walk. "One is what to do with Mrs. Ryder. The other is to find out what happened to the money Ryder got for his paintings."

"I thought Lestrade had already arrested Mrs. Ryder," I replied. "Indeed, I believe this is what you told Kern."

"I don't think I put it to Kern in such bald terms, Watson, but yes, I said it so he would get that impression. I wanted to know if he would come to her rescue, and found he would not. I believe I said that Lestrade was *detaining* her, which in a technical sense he did as he questioned her at her house as part of his official inquiry. Lestrade was fishing about for something, you can be sure of that. But he had no real evidence to push the matter into an arrest."

"And yet, Holmes, you have not told Lestrade all you know. If I didn't know better I might even say you seem reluctant to charge Mrs. Ryder with her husband's murder."

"But as you say, Watson, you *do* know better. Yes, she deserves to be punished for her crime, even if Cruelty urged upon her a vengeful spirit toward her husband."

"Then why not help Lestrade with the evidence?"

"Because someone does not want me to, and I must accede to their wishes." Holmes sighed and fell into a cryptic silence.

"And who is it, Holmes, that wishes a murderer to go free?" said I with some exasperation.

"The victim," said he, quietly.

"James Ryder? You're joking, Holmes!"

"Not at all. Soon everything will be explained. I have made an appointment with Mrs. Ryder, and we are overdue. Why the frown, Watson?"

"The idea of Kern and his sister both escaping justice for murdering Ryder is too much for me. There is still society's debt, Holmes."

"Yes, but that is Lestrade's job. I decline involvement this time."

"But you are hiding evidence! You have Mrs. Ryder's syringe in the apartment. How will Lestrade find it? It is unfair to the official police and, if I may say so, an action hardly within your character."

"No doubt in one sense you are right, Watson. But to a personal extent Lestrade, you, I, and everyone else *except* James Ryder, are in the same humble position. Upon that line of judgment of those who would accuse Mrs. Ryder, we cannot stand in front of him who has the greater claim."

"But James Ryder is dead. How can you know his wishes?"

"Patience, Watson! You yourself witnessed the man's last words. I am still working out in my mind the problem of approaching Mrs. Ryder. I hope to make a purchase from her late husband's estate, and if her guard is up she might refuse me. But at day's end I believe her punishment, if indeed we can call such measures punitive, will be an unusual one."

Holmes hailed a cab, and once more we began the lengthy ride across London to visit the lady in question.

"I gather then, Holmes," I said, trying to speak above the rattle of the carriage wheels, "that Rachel Ryder is no longer a suspect."

"That is correct, Watson. As I came to mull over the possibility of her involvement I realized she never would have told me about the torn Bible pages on the rubbish pile if she were using it as a hiding place for the syringe. That fact alone excludes her from further consideration. As simple as this deduction seems to me now, it did not occur to me for some time. And certainly no daughter could have wept so genuinely at her father's deathbed if such murderous guilt lay in her heart."

"I am glad to hear you say so, Holmes."

"Now before we arrive at Mrs. Ryder's, I want you to consider the last real puzzle in the Ryder case."

"The whereabouts of Ryder's money?"

"Precisely. I mean chiefly those proceeds he received by selling his entire work to Greeley. That was the bulk of his wealth. I have made inquiries, and apparently the lavish surroundings of his estate had been largely furnished upon credit, even down to some of the Master paintings. The bank must have been anticipating an enormous return in price after Ryder's tour of America and his expected exhibition at the New York Armory Show."

"One thought troubles me, Holmes. Do we really know if Ryder's paintings were actually sold? Could Kern have stolen them at the time of Ryder's death and then have lied about Greeley buying them?"

"No, I have verified the sale. I have gone to the office of the barrister who drew up Ryder's last will and testament. He was also present during the sale of Ryder's paintings to Greeley. The barrister remembers Greeley paying cash for the entire collection of canvases, and also recalls Ryder writing out a bill of sale for them. Kern and Greeley then loaded up the paintings into a van and congratulated Ryder upon his good fortune. The barrister admitted they brought a handsome price, but refused to reveal the exact amount to me.

"What immediately happened after Kern and his partner left is of equal interest. Ryder swore the barrister to secrecy and instructed him to transact some business for him. All the barrister would admit to me was that what he purchased was not for public sale. He did not tell me the cost. He carried out Ryder's wishes and provided him no further service. He believes all of Ryder's belongings, including what he was instructed to purchase, went to Mrs. Ryder immediately following Lestrade's investigation of the house. Mrs. Ryder and her daughter are the sole beneficiaries in the will, and we may assume they are now rich. But there is no currency. There have been no bank accounts, bonds, or stocks turned over to them. I suggested to Lestrade that he search the house carefully for any places in which money might have been hid, but he has come up empty. I am forced to conclude that Ryder must have used his money to buy some singular and unknown thing that in all probability is now at Mrs. Ryder's house."

"Unknown to us, you mean?"

"The barrister knows, of course. He is the only surviving witness."

"What could this object be, Holmes?"

"It is impossible to know for certain, and to blindly guess would be wasting time. But I have formed a theory. I will ask Mrs. Ryder a question to test my hypothesis. Though we will arrive there in a few moments, let me lay out the puzzle that has intrigued me for some days to see if you agree with my conclusions."

"Gladly, Holmes. I love a mystery."

"You will find this a knotty one, then. Do you recall Peter Vernet's conversation with James Ryder the day before Ryder died?"

"Yes, most of it. Maybe all of it."

"Then what do you think Ryder meant when he asked Vernet to tell me that the violin was the end of music for him."

I thought for a moment. "I would say, Holmes, that he knew that you, too, were a violin player, and that you shared the same appreciation for the instrument. As I think upon Ryder's statement that 'the violin is the end of music for me,' it reminds me of the popular saying, 'See Naples and die!' Both are cries of poetic exuberance. He is saying that the sound of the violin is the most beautiful experience to him."

"Good, Watson! A logical explanation, and perhaps right, so far as you state it. But remember Ryder's fussiness? He was anxious that Vernet relate the *exact* words. Why was that? Did he fear his poetic intention would be violated if he were not quoted exact, i.e., that some beauty in the words would be lost, or that the 'iambic' phrase, so to speak, would become the 'pentameter'? That seems a little ridiculous, doesn't it? After all, Ryder deserted his family. Does such a man worry about his prose being changed a little?"

"I understand your point, Holmes, and yet you must admit that artists are often very sensitive to colours, textures, shapes, and sounds, while remaining completely insensitive toward people."

Holmes laughed. "I agree, Watson. But do I detect an oblique reference to myself in your definition? For you say of me in one of your narratives, 'Artistic blood is liable to take the strangest forms.' "

"That was a compliment, Holmes. But I confess surprise. It appears you been reading my stories?"

"Just several," he said with a yawn. "In my more complicated investigations I have found it helps to become familiar with what is known to my antagonist. As Kern was so free in his reference to parts of your narratives, I decided to familiarize myself with some of them. So far it has not helped much, so my time has been was—er—that is, well spent in refamiliarizing myself with some of my older cases." Holmes suppressed another yawn. "I have spent a number of nights doing this."

"Any other conclusions?"

"None at all. Four nights of racking my brain over the entire matter has brought me no nearer to supposing what Ryder purchased. I can give no better explanation about the 'violin being the end of music' than you have just given in the last five minutes."

"You seem dissatisfied."

"Mind you, I see no evidence suggesting another possibility. However disconcerting it is that my conclusion matches your own, I am forced to accept it, at least for the moment. If we are right, it means that Ryder wanted me to know that he loved the sound of a violin. That is hardly surprising. Many people would choose some orchestral instrument as their favorite sound, and the violin is as popular as any other. Does this mean that he spent all of his proceeds on an expensive violin? That is a possibility. However, I should like to explore one other avenue. Let us suppose that he did not spend all of these proceeds on himself, but on someone else. For argument's sake, let us say this was his daughter."

"Why his daughter?"

"Practically speaking, she was the only family he ended up with—the only one who finally seems to have loved him without condition. So suppose he bought a gift that would please her. It might be different than a gift he would choose for himself—not a violin, but something else. She is a visual artist, and Ryder's ideal gift for her might have been an object of colour and shape, rather than one of sound. If with our relatively poor purses we were the ones attempting to buy the perfect gift for her, it might result in, say, a small watercolour by her favorite artist. But if Ryder had bought her a gift, it would have been something quite substantial."

"But Ryder himself was an artist. Why wouldn't he, too, have preferred colours and shapes to a violin?"

"He was no artist, Watson. Even by his own account his life was a forgery. Yet there is something to your objection, for a man who has so long played an actor's part to success can confuse that role with his real life. I believe at times Rider wished to go forth among the exotic to behold all that is called 'beautiful'—to 'See Ceylon and die', while at other times he felt that music was Beauty's best expression. But, in fact, Ryder never needed to have been torn between these two, for they each have their own beauty."

"As one woman is thought beautiful for her fair skin, while another is thought so because of her dark?"

"That would be another example, I suppose."

"I dimly see what you are saying, Holmes. Ryder's preference for art or music might depend on the moment and his mood."

"Excellent, Watson! And we will find out if our theory about a supreme gift for his daughter has any merit, for I hope to find this out at Mrs. Ryder's house, and here we are, unless I am much mistaken."

We left the carriage, and within the next moment Rachel Ryder had answered our knock and ushered us past the door and through the drawing room and hall, whereupon we entered a plainly furnished living room where stood the matron of the house and an elderly fat and bespectacled man named Mr. Horace, a dealer in antiques and sundries. In one corner of the room were stacks of boxes so high as to practically hide a grand piano that stood beyond them. The boxes were all marked, 'Ryder Estate'.

"I received your message, Mr. Holmes," said Elisabeth Ryder coldly. "I cannot confess to have understood it all."

Holmes smiled. "Not everyone is familiar with the language of diplomacy, Madame. I will hereafter be blunt so there is no confusion of meaning."

"I'm sorry Mr. Holmes. I didn't mean that *everything* in your letter was convoluted. You mentioned a cousin of yours who visited my husband and saw certain paintings in James's collection that you would like to purchase."

"Precisely, Madam. I am a great admirer of Sully and Gainsborough. To a lesser extent I like Constable and Turner, as well. I also enjoy Renaissance art. Apart from these I occasionally collect violins of a certain vintage."

"Constable and Turner, Mr. Holmes?" she replied, in the manner of an inquisitor. "Why, they are quite opposite in every respect. Most collectors champion one or the other. Might I ask why you prefer both?"

Holmes shrugged his shoulders and seemed lost for words. "I think because they painted such wonderful pictures," he stammered.

The woman snorted. "No doubt you do," she said. "Now tell me why you have really—"

"Of course, I disagree with Ruskin's view in the *Seven Lamps* that Turner's effects in oils, especially his central light sources, would not have been possible without his preparatory watercolours."

"What was that?" replied the woman blankly.

"But I was hoping today," added Holmes suavely, "to purchase something capturing the spirit of the Early to Middle Renaissance. Even well executed copies interest me."

"Oh, yes, of course," said Mrs. Ryder, regaining her composure.

"In particular I am given to believe that your husband had one or two excellent copies of the *Mona Lisa* ."

"Yes, I believe that is true. Their values are determined by Mr. Horace, who has been appraising and cataloguing all of the estate items for insurance."

Mr. Horace was a dealer in antiques and sundries

"May I see them?"

"There is only one copy, sir," bellowed Mr. Horace as he cleared his throat and set flapping the echoes of fleshy folds beneath his ponderous chin, "but its quality cannot be doubted. It is a fine forgery."

"Just the one copy, then?" inquired Holmes in a hoarse voice. I could see in the nuance of my companion's expression the deepest disappointment.

"How many copies does the gentleman *need*?" replied the old man with a perfect blend of seriousness and sarcasm.

"Right, then. Let us see the copy. Ah, yes, it is quite good. It was crated to prevent damage? That is splendid. By the way, what told you it was a forgery?"

The old man demurred with a false air of embarrassment. "*Experience*, Mr. Holmes," said he.

"And what does *experience* tell you it is worth?" replied my friend limply.

"One hundred ten, sir. Of course, the price would be more if the painting were not a recent work, as its quality is excellent."

Holmes tried to hide his shock. "Excuse me while I consult with my friend, Dr. Watson. This purchase is our first venture into art and is motivated by investment rather than sentiment."

The old man nodded while Holmes and I went to a corner of the room where our whispers could not be heard. "I was hoping, Watson," said he, as he leaned his hand upon the grand piano next to a stack of boxes and lightly tapped the wood twice for emphasis, "that we would find here *two* 'copies' of the *Mona Lisa*. I suppose it was a long shot for me to think that Ryder might have tried to buy the *Mona Lisa* on the black market as a supreme gift for his daughter. That was my hope. At least there is Vernet's copy. I think we should purchase it; Wolfgang Kern's original plan to retrieve the *Mona Lisa* is still dependent upon it. We will return it to cousin Vernet or to Director Bantok."

"Can you be sure of reimbursement, Holmes? Perhaps Lestrade could take care of it. Surely he could assume its possession on behalf of the French government?"

"I doubt that there is any official paperwork connecting the painting to its actual ownership by the Louvre as a work for hire."

"Can't the French museum just play out the scenario of 'finding' the *Mona Lisa*, here? Who would care if it were found at the house of Mr. Ryder or Mrs. Ryder?"

"There are a number of objections to playing the game that way, Watson. The chief obstacle, however, is that Vernet's copy has been legally conveyed to, and innocently received by, Mrs. Ryder. She is therefore the holder in ownership, and British probate law is pretty clear in such cases. Even stolen property would remain the ownership of Mrs. Ryder so long as she was unaware that it was stolen when it was conveyed to her. No, it is up to us to carry on with these shenanigans, Watson. We must purchase the painting. If the Louvre decided to 'find' it here, any connoisseur willing to pay Mrs. Ryder a few pounds to inspect the painting might discover it was a forgery. I'm confident of reimbursement. But I do wonder about the wisdom of the Louvre's plan if such an old man as Mr. Horace can see past Vernet's forgery so easily."

"I hate to think of it, Holmes, but this pompous fellow, Horace, seems to be the liaison to all the estate items and will probably be retained by the Yard to tell them what object it was into which Ryder dumped so much money."

"It depends on how far Lestrade carries his investigation into Ryder's death, Watson. It may end as a private matter, and the object we seek be forever hidden from us in one of these stacks and boxes. No, our visit here has hardly been inspiring. All that remains now is to give the undeserving Elisabeth Ryder her reprieve. Halloa! What is this?"

Holmes had been facing sideways to the piano near its row of keys when he cried out in a whisper, and he now leaned forward to see more clearly the sheet music laid open upon the hinged wooden support. His eyes glistened, and I followed his gaze to the last measure of the song. Then I looked up again at the intense, still expression sculpted into his features. Then his inscrutable gray eyes relaxed, and he turned toward Mrs. Ryder with a placid expression. "Watson and I have agreed to take the picture under one condition," said Holmes. "It demands a grand setting to surround it in case we do not sell it. I can think of nothing better than to hang it above such a fine instrument as this piano. Is it for sale?"

"The piano, for sale?"

"Yes."

"Certainly not, Mr. Holmes. This is not even part of the estate. It came with the house when I bought it, and I still play it. I have no desire to sell it."

"I do enjoy hearing mother play the piano," added Miss Ryder with an imploring look.

"Of course," said Holmes, doing his best to look disappointed. "I was only thinking how wonderful it would be to hear music again in my apartment—real music, I mean, not those gramophone records. I never realized how much I would miss the violin when I sold it soon after offering it to your daughter."

"I will see that the money you gave Rachel in lieu of the violin is returned to you, Mr. Holmes," said Elisabeth Ryder with disgust. "Then you can buy what *precious* violin you want."

"I categorically refuse the money's return, Madame."

"On the contrary, I insist—"

"Perhaps," interrupted Mr. Horace, "both the lady and the gentlemen would consider the sale of Mr. Ryder's violin from the estate."

"I didn't know my husband ever bought another violin," replied Mrs. Ryder.

"That is why *I* am here," said the wizened man. "*Everything* old around here has value," said he, with a touch of humor I thought not possible for him. He opened the case of the violin and held it up. "The violin and bow are in good condition," said he. "It was made for the Sears & Roebuck Company of Chicago. The instrument is not of professional quality, but would be sufficient for an experienced amateur."

"I believe *you* are an amateur, Mr. Holmes," said Mrs. Ryder, trying to sound matter-of-factly.

"What is the price?" asked my companion stiffly.

The old man resorted once more to his sheet. "Twelve pounds, three pence, sir."

"Three pence!" Holmes and I rejoined together involuntarily.

"No sirs, *Twelve pounds* and three pence."

"You are certain about the three pence then?" asked Holmes incredulously.

The old man lowered his glasses onto his nose and peered at Holmes and me with parental patience. "At Horace & Horace," he said in slow deliberate tones, "we endeavor to be *accurate,* so that no negotiation is necessary."

Holmes took out his purse with a rueful look. "At least you won't mind writing me a bill of sale, I suppose?"

"No mind at all," replied the old man, reaching out for Holmes's money with one hand and giving him a receipt with the other.

My friend pocketed the receipt. "There are a few other matters before I go, Mrs. Ryder, but the entire situation is most delicate," said he. "I must insist that I speak with you alone. No, Watson, you can stay."

To my surprise Mrs. Ryder, without protest, immediately dismissed Mr. Horace and her daughter to another room. She had apparently been anticipating Holmes's request, and she now stood stiffly before us with her hands collected into a bundle of interlaced fingers.

"What is it, then, Mr. Holmes?"

"I know that you poisoned your husband, Madame."

The woman's face went pale and her lip trembled.

"There is no use, Mrs. Ryder," added Holmes. "I have the hollowed-out Bible and the hypodermic syringe you used to inject poison into the wine. The syringe's diameter is rare in size and matches a corkstrand found in the bottle. I know that Wolfgang Kern is your brother, and that you discussed with him the murder of your husband."

Through an enormous effort the lady steadied her figure. "Where is my brother now?" she asked weakly.

"He is crossing the Atlantic."

"That is not possible. He wasn't going to New York until the fall. My father and he just mended their relationship."

"He won two tickets from Dr. Watson and I on a gamble. He's on that new luxury liner—what do they call it, Watson?"

"The *Titanic*, Holmes."

"Oh yes, that's it."

A profound hurt registered in Mrs. Ryder's eyes. "How could he leave without seeing me?" she cried. "My father and he were bitter with each other for so many years, and we are all a family again. I cannot think he is gone—why did he not see me before he left?"

"He did not say, Madame. But certainly he was astonished when I told him of your guilt."

The lady appeared stunned and her body began to sway. She fell heavily onto the sofa, and her moistened eyes welled up with tears. No doubt she thought of her brother who had fled aghast at the news of her, and now Holmes, too, knew what she had done. Another moment passed as a wave of despair engulfed her, and she wept in anguish as the pitch of her moaning rose and fell in intense grief. At one point she seemed beside herself and held her head in her hands while rocking her body to and fro. Holmes, however, was unmoved by the woman's paroxysm of despair, and it was a long time before the woman spoke.

"What are you going to do with me, Mr. Holmes?" she finally managed to stutter in sobs as she raised her tear-stained face.

"Your husband has given me instructions to that end, Madame," said Holmes. "I told your husband that I believed you were his murderer just before he died. He said what should be done, and I have decided to follow his wishes." Holmes paused and the lady's hands clasped and unclasped before her, while her reddened face and clenched teeth screwed up into a weird, pinched look of anxiety. Then for some seconds the shock of the previous moment caused her to assume an eerie stillness. Despite the petrified and tangled thoughts that threatened to fragment her mind she wanted to hear clearly the verdict uttered by her dead husband. She would hear it, however fateful, however final.

"An orderly was there," Madame," continued Holmes. "And so was Dr. Watson. They will attest to what he said. Your husband's voice was hardly audible, but he did his best to mouth some words: " 'Forgive her,' or 'Forget her,' —we're not sure which. At any rate I am granting your husband's wishes."

It took a moment for the woman to understand that her life was spared. Then her head dropped and she wept uncontrollably, her shoulders heaving up and down in unison with her bobbing head. "Oh, thank you Mr. Holmes." she managed.

"I hardly think you deserve much pity, Mrs. Ryder," remarked my friend. "Because of you, your daughter nearly lost both of her parents—one to murder, the other to jail if not the hangman's noose. She now has but one parent left, and a murderer at that."

"Please don't tell her, Mr. Holmes. Please don't," she cried.

Her begging was pitiful, and I marveled at the transformation of this woman. Now wallowing in emotion, she was hardly recognizable as the same person who a moment before could not speak peaceably with Holmes.

"Your punishment will be of a different sort, Mrs. Ryder," added Holmes sternly. "You will always live with the knowledge that your husband knew of your murderous deed against him, but forgave you anyway. You blamed him during the last twelve years for being absent from your daughter, and now you can blame yourself for his absence in all the years that follow. In the end he became a decent man, a better human being than yourself."

For some time the woman's grief was so extraordinary that even Holmes stopped lecturing her. Finally, as the grief-ridden wailing motion of the woman's frame began to subside, Holmes finished his verdict.

"I leave you as I left your husband years ago," continued he. "I gave him an open door, a second chance to redeem what was left of his life. Apparently it was his desire that you receive the same opportunity."

The woman held her head down, ashamed, and silent.

"There is one other small matter before I go," said Holmes. He lifted his newly purchased violin out of the case and held it flat with the palms of his hands beneath it, as a soldier might bear a comrade's corpse from a battlefield of sacrifice. "I grant your husband's wish, Mrs. Ryder, and free you in more serious circumstances than those in which I once freed him. I do it because he valued mercy so. The ends of a man's life do not justify its means, but I believe your husband did his best to redeem your future, and also to redeem, as much as was possible, more than just the last moment of his life when he asked for your clemency."

"What, then?" she gasped through her tear-soaked voice.

"*His past,*" said Holmes. Rolling his left wrist carefully around the neck of the violin and his other around the chin rest Holmes made a sudden motion downward and shattered the violin upon his knees. The catgut strings, bridge, and parts of the neck and tailpiece, the very *disjecta membra* of the violin, lay awry about him. Through all this Holmes had held fast the two ends of the instrument, and he now addressed the woman as he turned the severed neck of the violin around to reveal a large brilliant jewel hidden inside a carved-out niche. "The last time I saw this stone, Madame, was thirteen years ago when I handed it back to its former owner, the Countess of Morcar, just after I had caught your husband stealing it. It remained with her until she died. The Countess's daughter who inherited it was always superstitious about the misfortune that followed its owners. When it recently became hers she let it be known privately that the gem was for sale. Your husband learned of it last week and sold his life's work to purchase it."

I heard Mrs. Ryder gasp, and we both looked in astonishment at the sight of the priceless stone. She instinctively reached forward to touch the jewel, but stopped shy of the mark and slowly retrieved her hand.

Holmes placed the broken pieces of the fiddle back in its case and gestured that I not forget Vernet's copy of the *Mona Lisa* propped upon the arms of a chair.

"Your husband wished that this violin be given to Rachel. As I am now its owner I will have the violin repaired and given to her. I will also have the jewel sold and its entire value put into a trust fund for her benefit—to be drawn upon annually. In the event of an untimely death, your daughter's trust fund will belong to the orphanage at St. Matthias Church."

"You really don't trust me at all, do you, Mr. Holmes?" said Elisabeth Ryder with a deep, sad, questioning gaze.

My companion's eye was steady upon her, and his voice was calm and even. "No, Madame," he said. "I do not."

Without further comment Holmes turned away, and I hurried after him as he walked out the door.

Chapter Nine

It was a fortnight later when I visited Sherlock Holmes at his modest cabin that overlooked the Dover Cliffs. He had come to his one room abode after cabling his publisher in America to postpone his visit, and now he set himself to study his honeybees that had become active again in the warm winds of spring. His material wants were few, and an old neighborly woman and her grandson took care of them. The only place the old woman refused to serve his meals was an outbuilding behind the cabin, a simple structure which served, in effect, as one huge beehive. It was the kind of sanctuary for which Holmes had long sought. It was a simple rectangular shed with a roof, except it was completely open upon the northern end for light. And in his own way Holmes was still in his element, except that, instead of living on Baker Street in the midst of a great city surrounded by people and buildings, he now (each day after breakfast) sat inside this shed surrounded by walls made up of bees jostling against one another inside stacks of beehive boxes. The inside wall of each hive was made of glass, so that the bees were visible from within the shed, and Holmes would roll about on a movable chair taking notes and drawing diagrams of any one of a hundred apiaries. It was an observer's paradise, and here Holmes stayed for whole afternoons at a time.

To sit and talk with my friend surrounded by the sound of ten thousands of bees was a bit unnerving, however, so Holmes agreed to postpone his latest experiment of exposing the insects to changes in coloured light based on the rhythm and harmonies of American Negro music recorded on gramophone records, and agreed to some quiet conversation with me in his cabin. After a variety of subjects Holmes launched into a discussion of the synestesia of the Russian composer Scriabin and its affects upon that composer's compositions. Not until he divulged himself entirely on this subject did I hand him a month's worth of the public prints.

"I heard about the *Titanic*, Watson," said he, as he shuffled through some issues of the Globe. "I didn't realize the tragedy was so immense."

"Everyone in London was equally amazed, Holmes. I thought it best to wire the port authority in New York to see if our names, or those of Wolfgang Kern or Jonah Greeley, were listed as survivors. They were not."

"Ah, I have been wondering about that."

"I included our names in case Kern and Greeley never registered under their own."

"And the entire collection of James Ryder's paintings?"

"Only one piece of luggage was salvaged from the ship. There was nothing special about its contents; just some socks, shirts, and underclothes."

Holmes brought out his familiar pipe. "I might have thought that wooden crates and wooden-framed pictures would have floated on the sea. But no doubt they went down within the bowels of the sinking ship."

"I read in the *Globe,* Holmes, that witnesses saw some letters and small packages floating up from below 'G' deck where the mail was stored, but that was all."

"So Kern and Greeley and the lifetime work of James Ryder have ended up on the bottom of the cold Atlantic."

"Along with fifteen hundred other people, Holmes."

"It might have been us there, Watson. One thinks of that moment when Wolfgang Kern was in our apartment and chose the lot. We thought only *his* life lay in the balance, but we never suspected ours lay there, too. Imagine the feeling of terror that would have been ours had we known then, as we know now, of the even odds being waged for our deaths as the marble was pushed out from the pouch. And to think that we felt dismay upon seeing the white marble! Black would have meant death for us both. And yet, Watson, every man on the frigid *Titanic* who gave up his seat on a lifeboat must have experienced an even more poignant feeling than would have we in our apartment, choosing voluntarily, as it were, a black marble for himself so that another might have the white. No greater sacrifice can be imagined. Yet these same men with such noble deeds perished alongside the murderer Wolfgang Kern. I know that time and chance happens to all men, but sometimes these forces seem absurd to me."

"I agree, Holmes. One of these papers has a clergyman's response to the many who have asked where God was in the midst of this tragedy. It ends by suggesting that if all men got their just and immediate desserts for their lives, then even the best of mankind would perish in a day. I found it a rather bleak view."

"The Good Book never pretended to have any other view, Watson—not after its first few chapters, at least. But the question is deeper than you suppose. I am sure the clergyman would maintain that the importance of his view is not whether it is bleak, but whether it is true."

"I thought his tone insensitive."

"Well, it's a hard saying. He might have picked a different way to say it, though I wouldn't judge him too harshly if he includes himself in the sweep. To be sure, these are days when men should also cheer these others for their courage."

"The prime minister called it their *'Titanic'* courage."

"Indeed!"

"But speaking of tragedy, Holmes, and as I think of Kern and Greeley steaming out to their fate upon the deck of the *Titanic*, I must admit I have never been clear about certain points in the Ryder case."

"Anything in particular?"

"I was astonished at how you knew that Ryder had used the violin to hide the carbuncle. This is uppermost of many questions I have."

"Well, Watson," he said with a laugh, "I can't have my biographer mystified over one of the more intriguing cases of late. Let me see if I can give you a brief account of the events as I understood them. We will prove Kern wrong after all, and include this case among the annals! It is especially possible to do so now, for I have talked at length with Vernet and have also received a lengthy response from my letter to Mrs. Ryder asking her for clarification on certain trifling details. She could hardly refuse this request as coming from one of her benefactors.

"The sequence of events regarding James Ryder began, of course, when Rachel Ryder came to us because her father seemed to have disappeared from the hotel where he was temporarily staying. His letter and telegram to her were too genuine in feeling to suppose he had merely returned to his country villa without explanation. As it turned out, the reason for his disappearance was a fairly simple one—he had been arrested. The police had arrived at the Commonds Hotel and taken him away on a charge of stealing the Botticelli painting, which rendering was, in fact, a mere forgery of the Botticelli by my cousin, Peter Vernet. Ryder had no way to get word to his daughter about his arrest, and, if he did, he may not have wanted her to know about it. He was innocent and no doubt hoped he would be cleared of the charge before his daughter learned of his arrest in the papers. Had she read of his arrest, it might have suggested to her that her father was not so reformed as she had guessed from his correspondence. The actual culprit in all this was Director Bantok of the Louvre. From the very beginning Vernet suspected that the Director had used his Botticelli copy to bring a false charge against Ryder. The Director was the only one with whom Vernet had discussed his egg-tempera copy of the original Botticelli that hung in the Louvre, and Verent also knew the Director had great antipathy toward Ryder's art. Once Vernet finished the copy, it would be a simple matter for the Director, some evening when he was alone, to hide the original Botticelli painting in his office and then take Vernet's copy from the museum and put it into the hotel room where Ryder was staying."

"Why didn't he just use the original, Holmes?"

"He could have, but even an hour's risk of fire or theft to the original would likely have convinced him not to use it."

"And how did the Director get past the locked door of Ryder's suite?"

"The Director needed an ally—a confederate maid or a clerk at the desk. These people are notoriously underpaid in their positions and are most susceptible to a little pecuniary persuasion. I have myself made ample use of this fact over the years. The Director had learned about Ryder's criminal past from Wolfgang Kern, who in turn had learned it from your original Blue Carbuncle story, and the Director judged correctly that it would prejudice the police against him. So he contacted Scotland Yard in an anonymous telegram accusing Ryder of having stolen the Botticelli. There is irony here, for Ryder himself once exploited someone's criminal history to direct attention away from himself. Anyway, much to the delight of the Director, James Ryder was arrested and removed from the scene. Because the Director hated Ryder's work he loathed the idea of the Louvre purchasing it. Vernet claims that Bantok wanted the Louvre to be safe from the *infidels* until his retirement.

"But Vernet was troubled about the arrest of Ryder, and discussed his suspicions about the Director with a few members of the Louvre's museum board. After Ryder's death these members (who were more fair-minded than their director), became concerned that Bantok might further damage Ryder's legacy by giving another anonymous tip to the police, this time claiming that another painting, the *Mona Lisa,* was at Ryder's villa. After all, why would the Director care about Ryder's death? As far as he was concerned it was still an opportunity to put into motion Kern's plan for the recovery of the *Mona Lisa.*"

"What kind of punishment will the Director bear for his part in all this, Holmes?"

"I will come to that in a moment, Watson. We can thank Rachel Ryder, though, for being able to provide us with a sketch of the Director. Bantok's presence at Ryder's apartment in London remains a mystery to me, but perhaps he believed there were some compromising letters that could damage Ryder's reputation. As for the Botticelli, the only other person who had access to both renditions of it was my cousin Vernet, and he was never a suspect. Simply put, I have known him all of his life, have witnessed his integrity innumerable times, and know he could not have been any more guilty than you or I.

"In fact, Vernet was quite helpful to us throughout the case. He told us of Ryder's arrest, and of Ryder's life on Ceylon, when the man tried to recast himself as an artist. Ryder was little more than a simpleton when we first met, but his creativity showed even then. No dullard would have thought to hide a jewel in the belly of a goose. This trait in Ryder was the one forte in his personality, and he did his best to exploit it during his life. Of his own life and work in Ceylon we have his own testimony. What we must add is the effect of his art upon the eccentric set in Europe. It was electric. I have it on Vernet's authority that Ryder's art was being sought by a growing number of influential collectors. But then this personal tragedy occurred to Ryder in Ceylon.

"With this trial Ryder came to contemplate the insincerity of his life, and he had a fundamental change in heart. His associate, Wolfgang Kern, also underwent change, but in a different way. The latter had been an outcast in his family when he was a young man because of a passage with a woman whom he refused to marry. The girl's father and Kern's father were best of friends, and old man Kern excoriated his son for his behavior. Young Wolfgang, as I shall continue to call him, became so removed from his family that James Ryder never met him during the whole of his life with Elisabeth. Nevertheless, Kern heard from a friend that Ryder had deserted to Ceylon, and he decided to approach his sister and offer his help in raising the children. She agreed, and he moved in with her. During the course of the next several years his nephew died, and his sister found out about his addition to the drug. She feared his negative influence upon her daughter, but he soon departed anyway. Severed then for Kern was that last connection he had with his family, and he soon decided to follow his brother-in-law overseas and live the life of a vagabond.

When he met Ryder in Ceylon Kern pretended he was only a distant relative of Ryder's wife, and he made an impromptu change in his first name from Walter to Wolfgang. He was unable to change his surname because Ryder had chanced to be painting a watercolour at the dock when the he saw a trunk marked 'W. Kern' and made himself known to the man who carried it off. Why Kern changed his first name is unclear, but probably he wanted his whereabouts kept secret from his family. Eventually Kern perceived from his conversations with Ryder that the break between his sister and Ryder was so great that no correspondence passed between them, and so his identity remained hidden. In the end, Kern's self-exile proved more effective than even he could have guessed, for after twelve years away from England he actually failed to recognize his own niece in a photograph.

"Life continued uneventful for Kern until more than a decade later, when James Ryder suffered the loss of his concubine and son. Ryder decided to return to England, and Kern went with him. Shortly afterward Kern visited his sister Elisabeth whom he had not seen in a dozen years. His niece was away visiting a relative at the time, and she and Kern, by all rights, should have reunited in Lestrade's carriage. That is why Kern wore his muffler tight against his face during his ride and visit to the hospital, for he was afraid his niece might cry out in recognition of him and thereby cause Lestrade to wonder at the newspaper's description of him as only a distant relation to Mrs. Ryder.

"At any rate, after renewing his acquaintance with his sister, Kern told her he was upset that Ryder wanted to sell his paintings to the Louvre before the New York Armory Show took place. He had argued with Ryder that entrance into the show would increase the paintings' value by at least fifty percent, but Ryder seemed not to care. However, Ryder agreed to sell his share of interest in the paintings. Kern scrambled without success to find an investor to buy out Ryder in the immediate days that followed. (Not before some weeks would pass would he find in Greeley a collector willing to invest in an entire collection of unconventional art.)

"He and his sister Elisabeth then talked of her life, and Kern became further incensed against Ryder upon hearing of the deprivation caused by his brother-in-law's desertion. Kern, of course, had been a ne'er-do-well, but like so many of his kind he came to excuse himself for the same faults of which he thought others should be held accountable. So angry did he become during his conversation with his sister that he mused about poisoning her husband. Brother and sister soon found themselves planning impromptu the murder of Ryder in detail, for Mrs. Ryder had often fantasized about killing her husband if given the opportunity.

"It was Mrs. Ryder's idea that the murder could be done by injecting diluted arsenic into a series of wine bottles that would then be drunk by her husband over a period of several months. In this way she hoped to avoid suspicion. They even discussed the exact amount of poison to be divided into two-dozen bottles of wine. One of the problems, however, lay in administering the poison. Kern had arranged a two-month journey to promote Ryder's work in galleries all over Europe, and therefore could not be on hand to poison each bottle after it was opened. The poison would have to be put into the bottles before he left. Then he remembered the hypodermic needle he had borrowed that very day, and he mentioned it to his sister. She, too, had access to a syringe, but she kept this fact hidden from her brother. Of course, the combined acts of both caused the evidence of the corkstrands."

"Just a minute, Holmes," said I. Why didn't they insert the needle between the edge of the cork and the neck of the bottle? This way no evidence of corkstrands would have been left inside the wine."

"Inserting the needle there would have put more pressure on the glass, Watson, and possibly have caused the bottles to crack. The cork, too, would not have resumed its shape upon its edge as likely as it would have closed upon a puncture in its center, and a positive seal to the wine had to be maintained. As for the presence of corkstrands, that was never much of a concern to Kern, who knew Ryder was not in the habit of pouring out the last dregs from a bottle. After much discussion of the whole matter Elisabeth tried to persuade her brother that they ought not to act. But secretly she resolved to poison the bottles herself. Little did she know that her brother had merely pretended to be dissuaded.

"Mrs. Ryder waited for her brother to leave on his two-month journey and then contacted her husband. She proposed a visit to discuss their daughter's future in art. He agreed, and hoped for some form of reconciliation with her. Their meeting was a cool one, however. She had hardly arrived when she asked to retire to a room because of feeling ill from the journey. From this room she was able to reach the cellar without notice, and she poisoned the bottles using her syringe. The whole affair took less than an hour, and she returned to Ryder in the grand room saying she felt much better. Their conversation was brief, and both agreed that Ryder would support his daughter if she could gain entrance into a university. Mrs. Ryder hastened her leave but promised to provide the exact cost of their daughter's education for the coming year."

"What was Mrs. Ryder's purpose then, Holmes, in going with Dr. Stenerude to visit her husband?"

"It was a blind, Watson, put there mostly for our sake. It gave the appearance that Mrs. Ryder wanted to see her husband whom she claimed she had not seen since his return to England. And in the kindly esteemed doctor she also had a formidable witness to the fact that she left the doctor's carriage before having had an opportunity to poison her husband's medications. Then too, from the viewpoint of James Ryder, it might seem a natural part of his reconciliation with his wife that she thaw in her attitude enough to want to visit him again, even if it was mainly for their daughter's sake. This would help disarm any suspicions he might have against her if his symptoms from poisoning caused him to think back upon her visit. Incidentally, I have never corrected Mrs. Ryder about her belief that she acted alone. I decided her sense of guilt might be greater if she remained ignorant of her brother's role. What result this will bear in her life remains to be seen.

As for Mrs. Ryder's plan, it might have worked had we not found other evidences against her. We discovered, for example, the hollowed out Bible with the actual syringe used in the murder, as well as a child's book with her maiden name which showed me the connection to her brother. We also found the set of books about Napoleon and a copy of the Anglo Journal of Medicine, the monthly periodical which her father gave her each month when he was finished reading it. We get this same magazine at our apartment *pro bono* because of your medical ties, Watson, and I saw an article in a previous issue by experts who have come to believe in recent years that Napoleon was poisoned. I knew that Mrs. Ryder had an abiding interest in biographical history, including the Emperor, that she had a hypodermic syringe at her disposal, and that she had read the only book in a set on Napoleon which, in fact (I have checked it out), discusses theories about whether or not the Emperor was murdered, and how it was done. Mrs. Ryder assimilated all this into her plan.

"And the Bible, Holmes? I don't remember seeing you take it off the shelf."

"Before Mrs. Ryder entered the room, I misdirected you to a picture frame while I slipped the Bible into a very large inner pocket of my loose-fitting overcoat. Should Mrs. Ryder have noticed her family Bible missing, she might suspect it was secreted upon my person if she saw your uneasiness."

"I see."

"It was while we were interviewing Mrs. Ryder that Lestrade arrived with the catastrophic news that James Ryder was dying. His health had declined at an alarming rate, and I think you would agree that his anxiety over his arrest probably hastened his death. His hospitalization provoked such startled and genuine reactions from Mrs. Ryder and her brother, Wolfgang Kern, however, that I briefly considered whether the whole of my theory about these siblings was wrong. But other evidences pointed to their guilt. So I asked myself if there were any circumstances under which they could be guilty of his murder, yet dismayed at his sickness. One possibility occurred to me. If each had poisoned the bottles without the other knowing it, Ryder would have become sick much sooner than either of them expected. That would explain their surprise. And if Ryder's doctor at the hospital diagnosed his symptoms correctly the police would be informed, and perhaps they themselves be sought as suspects in his poisoning. Their worry, then, could be because of the *suddenness* of Ryder's illness, rather than the illness itself. The fact that Mrs. Ryder and her brother had access to their own syringes then struck me afresh. Perhaps the needles were not the same and left their own distinctive 'calling card'. Examining any of the remaining bottles to see if they contained two corkstrands of slightly different diameters could test my theory. The test proved positive, and my evidence was nearly complete."

"But why did you think it was Kern and not Director Bantok who had poisoned the bottles? You've already noted, Holmes, how much the Director hated Ryder's work, and how he feared he might be forced to purchase it for the Louvre. He even had Ryder arrested on a false charge and sent to prison."

"What you say is true, Watson. A question remains as to whether the Director ever had the same opportunity to poison James Ryder as did Kern or Mrs. Ryder. But if he did have the opportunity he never made use of it. I examined the tops of all the corks and the only colour of paint I found was blue. When Kern pushed the needle all the way through the Velasquez painting it apparently caught some of the minute crazing, of which a small speck adhered to the hip of the piston. It redeposited itself the next time the syringe was used, which was when Kern injected the poison into the first of all the bottles. The Director, if you remember, believed that *green* paint was to be tested. Kern, therefore, and not the Director, had been using the syringe immediately prior to using it on the bottles."

"But perhaps the Director poisoned the bottles without leaving any traces of green paint, Holmes. After all, there were two strands."

"No, Watson. The second strand could not belong to the Director because the diameter of the strands in the bottle would then be the same. Kern used the Director's syringe, if you remember."

"Incredible!" I said, shaking my head in amazement. "A reasoning *tour de force!* I suppose all that is left, Holmes, is to tell me how you came to astonish us all by knowing the Blue Carbuncle was hidden inside the violin."

"I am grateful to you on that point, Watson. Had it not been for your attention to extraneous minutia, a habit of yours over which I have often despaired, I would not have recalled my own memories of the exact type of tail markings found on the goose into which James Ryder first hid the jewel so many years ago. The tail had a double-bar marking across its tail feathers. This detail proved essential to the case. That fact was not in my conscious mind as I stared absent-mindedly at the sheet music on Mrs. Ryder's piano while wondering how to dicker with Mr. Horace. Then suddenly I saw the answer to Ryder's cryptic statement—there was a double bar at the end of the music. Each measure in a musical piece has but one vertical line spanning the staff, but there is always the symbol of double bar lines at the end of the last measure. Ryder had said that the violin was the end of music to him. This was an encrypted way of saying that the violin was the *'double bar'* to him, i.e. *that the violin was the goose to him*. He had once used a goose to hide the Blue Carbuncle. So this time he had apparently hid it in a violin."

"Amazing Holmes!"

"Rudimentary, really."

But why didn't he tell your cousin Vernet to relay this information to you? Why the elaborate deception?"

"Don't forget, Watson, that at stake was the Blue Carbuncle. And while he might tell his life story to Vernet, my cousin was still a relative stranger to him. The jewel was another matter; Ryder did not know him *that* well. So he asked Vernet to give me a message in the event he was unable to get the violin to his daughter."

"Incredible, Holmes! I looked upon the same sheet music as you, but with never a thought of its connection. The jewel would still be lost if you had not deduced the hidden meaning of Ryder's statement."

"I have since seen Ryder's barrister to tell him I discovered the gem. He seemed amused at the whole affair of my discovery and asked about the painting I bought at Mrs. Ryder's. He had learned of the picture's sale from Mr. Horace."

"I meant to ask you about that, Holmes. What happened to it?"

"Oh, Vernet has his copy back. Technically the Louvre owns it, and has temporarily entrusted it to his keeping. I have a mind to buy it, however."

"I'm a little lost, Holmes. I was with you when you bought Vernet's copy from Mrs. Ryder. And apparently you have given it to Vernet, for you say you now want to buy it from him. But where is the sense? You purchased it so that you could give it to Vernet, so that you could purchase it, again?"

"I do want to buy Vernet's copy, Watson. It will all be clear to you within the hour, but let me give you a partial explanation now. When I told the barrister I was about to return the painting to Vernet, he wore a strange smile and gave a curious reply."

" 'How,' asked he, 'can you return a thing to someone if he already has it?'

" 'What do you mean?' I asked.

" 'Did no one tell you that the Director of the Louvre had Inspector Lestrade retrieve your cousin's copy of the *Mona Lisa* out of Ryder's villa as soon as he heard that Ryder had died?'

" 'Then what copy is it that I have? Ah!—'

"'Yes, that's right, Mr. Holmes. You own the *Mona Lisa!* I purchased both the Blue Carbuncle and the *Mona Lisa* with the proceeds from Ryder's sale to Greeley. Ryder asked me to find out if the *Mona Lisa* had ever been made available. I knew some persons who have associations with the black market, and one of them specializes in art. It turned out that the *Mona Lisa* had just come to the 'market' within days. Apparently the thief had been violently sick for weeks when he finally realized it was due to nervous exhaustion and from months of fearing he would be captured with the *Mona Lisa.* So the da Vinci had surfaced, and it was being offered for a relatively good price. Ryder had me buy it and planned to deliver it to the Louvre in the presence of the Director and some newspapermen."

"It was not bought for his daughter, then?"

"No. He wanted the world to understand his newfound integrity, and he believed the *Mona Lisa* belonged to the public. Unfortunately, it was while he was organizing this effort that his health collapsed. He asked that I deliver the painting on his behalf to the Louvre, should he die before being able to do so himself. By the time I learned of his death, however, it was a few days after Lestrade's investigation, and Mrs. Ryder had already taken everything of Ryder's to her own house. Her action was not apropos, but as the estate all passed into Elisabeth and Rachel's hands, anyway, there was little to which I could legally object. Through an agent I made immediate contact with her, for I feared she might learn of my connection to her husband and refuse to sell me the painting. But you beat us to the punch, Mr. Holmes. So I congratulate you on owning the *Mona Lisa.*'

"And that is how, Watson, I became the owner of the da Vinci."

"You're joking, Holmes!"

My companion bent down and pressed his fingers into a crevice of the floorboards. Presently a section of pine planks that were nailed together lifted up, and he slid the panel to one side.

"This is the painting?" I asked in disbelief, pointing to a wrapped package he now drew from a recess in the floor. "This is the *Mona Lisa?* Holmes, this is too unbelievable!"

"Here it is, Watson," said he, unwrapping the picture to show me the most priceless art object known to man.

"It is Wonderful! Wonderful!" I cried, throwing my hands into the air. I sat in raptured astonishment for a long time as Holmes examined it carefully. Then he replaced it in the packaging, laid it on the bed, and put the section of floorboards back over the hole.

"Holmes," said I, when I finally found my voice, "My readers will think I am concocting stories when I write up this case!"

"This tale is not over, Watson. I am expecting two visitors shortly, and I wanted you here as my witness when they arrive. That was why I asked you to come during the week. Ah, here they come now."

I looked out the window and saw two gentlemen struggling up the hill toward Holmes's cabin, for there was no road leading up from the foot of the hill. One of these men was Lestrade, and the other I recognized from Rachel Ryder's sketch.

"I got your message, Holmes," cried Lestrade as he stopped and stood some yards from the cabin to catch his breath. "I have brought Director Bantok to share your hopes. He would like to commence as soon as possible, though I believe he is in need of some salve for a sting received by one of your infernal bees."

"Excellent," remarked Holmes. "Come in!"

The men took off their coats and seated themselves in some rustic wooden chairs near the roughly hewn brownstone fireplace, and Holmes sat on a small stool opposite them. I took a chair between them facing the hearth.

"I understand, Mr. Holmes," began the Director mopping his brow, "that you have some news regarding the whereabouts of the *Mona Lisa*. I am exceedingly glad. I swore to myself when it was stolen that I would not rest until its return. In fact, I promised the officers at the Louvre that I would delay my retirement until the *da Vinci* was restored to the Museum."

"It was stolen during your watch, Monsieur?"

"Yes, Mr. Holmes. But even the Director cannot be in all places at all times. Every precaution was taken against such a crime, I assure you."

"Of course," replied Holmes. "You are most anxious for its recovery, then?"

"Certainly!"

"Then I am happy to report I have tracked the painting to its lair. I have also had a connoisseur look at it. I don't know the identity of the thief, but the painting itself is currently housed in a disreputable abode, hardly better than a shack. I think we must move quickly. The owner of the place is a conniving sort of fellow, though. We must act with care."

"We are all attention, Mr. Holmes."

"The painting recently came onto the black market, and this crafty fellow has somehow gotten hold of it. His demands are very peculiar, but, on the whole, I think them rather generous."

"Go on, Mr. Holmes. The suspense is killing us!"

"Very good. He asks in exchange for the *Mona Lisa* a painting of his choice from the Museum."

"That is not so bad," replied the Director. "The *Mona Lisa* for any other painting in the Museum is a bargain. We have works of Rembrandt and Vermeer, Claude and Poussin and Rubens. Titian even!"

"Unfortunately his preference is toward the earlier Renaissance. His taste actually runs along similar lines to that of the thief."

"We have Giotto and Botticelli, then. Would these do? *The Disciples Casting Their Nets* is a seminal work in vanishing point perspective—more groundbreaking than the *Mona Lisa*, really."

"Actually he prefers da Vinci in particular."

"Da Vinci?" The Director threw up his hands. "What kind of game is this? Other than the *Mona Lisa* we only have da Vinci's questionable attribution—the angel of the *Madonna Of The Rocks*."

"He is not so particular as that. He has heard there is a brilliant copy of the *Mona Lisa* by the young artist, Peter Vernet."

"He wants a copy?"

"Yes."

"I must not be understanding you, Mr. Holmes. Are you saying that this man has the authentic *Mona Lisa*, but that he will exchange it for a *copy*?"

"Yes, that's right."

"Is he mad?"

"I think he would prefer the term 'eccentric'."

The Director sat back with amazement written across his features. "I thought I had seen it all. And you say a connoisseur has verified it?"

"A connoisseur named Mr. Horace has looked at it."

"Oh, I know him," replied the Director. "He is a brilliant man, a genius, really. No one is better at attribution."

"You agree to exchange the painting, then?"

"If you think this strange man is serious, Mr. Holmes. Yes, of course!"

"Oh, he is serious, all right. But he has a few other conditions that must be met."

"And what are those, Mr. Holmes?"

"First, that you keep these proceedings secret."

"I am a man of honour, sir," replied the Director with offended dignity.

"Very well. He also requests that a one-line announcement be read to the public upon the renewed unveiling of the *Mona Lisa*."

"Certainly, Mr. Holmes. What is it?"

"I have it here," said my companion opening up a small piece of paper which from my unique vantage point I saw was blank. "It reads as follows: *'The Director of the Louvre, Mssr. Bantok, is a jack-in-box.'*

"What?" cried the Director as he sprang from his seat and threw out his hands. "Are you joking, Mr. Holmes!"

"Well, I did say he was eccentric."

The Director resumed his seat and his body seemed to shrink before our very eyes. "And what else does he want?" he squeaked.

"He will not return the *Mona Lisa* unless you first retire. And he promises to return it within eighteen months."

A look of vexation and defeat passed across the Director's haggard face. "Then I will be unable to keep my promise to the officers of the Louvre," he said sadly. "If it were not for my love of da Vinci, I should never subject myself to such humiliation. Nevertheless, I agree to his terms, Mr. Holmes. Please see that he gets this message."

"Consider it done," replied my friend.

"There is one more thing, Mr. Holmes. This is a very queer business, and I should like to be certain that this bizarre fellow has really empowered you to accept his terms. I don't doubt he has instructed you, but how can we know he will keep faith with us? After all, I wouldn't want to retire and then find I had been hoaxed."

"He has left me a double pledge."

"What exactly?"

"Here is a typewritten copy of his demands," said Holmes, taking a folded sheet of paper from his pocket. "He has signed it below."

"Rummy! That's the worse signature I've ever seen—I can't even read his name! What kind of pledge is that?"

"I grant that the other is more convincing."

"Never mind, Mr. Holmes. I think I shall be done with this. I am certain now this associate of yours is a fool, and that he has been playing a joke on us all."

"At least consider the second pledge before you go," said Holmes, reaching for the package on the bed and unwrapping it.

"Very well, if I must. But I really don't see—"

The Director paused and stared at the painting that Holmes now held in front of him. His mouth fell agape and locked in a catatonic-like trance, and a moment passed before he seemed to regain even a sense of his own presence. Then he instinctively snatched the picture out of Holmes's hands and held it in front of him. He peered at it closely, especially its edging, then held it back again at arm's length and looked at each of us in turn.

"This is it!" cried he. "It is she! It is the true *Mona Lisa!*"

"Yes," said Holmes, reaching over and gingerly lifting the painting out of the upturned hands of the stunned Director. "It is indeed."

"I can't believe it. I can believe it. It is here! It is no dream! This is wonderful! *Just wonderful!*" sang the Director. He laughed in a merry daze and his hands slapped down upon his thighs. "No better pledge could be given you, Mr. Holmes," said he, sputtering. "The *Mona Lisa* will be recovered by the Louvre. And I will not be disgraced forever."

Holmes re-wrapped the painting and placed it back on his bed. "I believe this concludes our business," said he.

"Yes, yes," cried the Director, still beside himself with emotion, "you can go back to your bees, now, Mr. Holmes. Can't keep the little fellows waiting, you know. Thank you! Thank you so much!"

The two men left the cabin and the voice of the happy Director could still be heard from lower on the hill as Holmes crouched down upon the floor to replace the painting into its hiding place.

"I was fairer than I should have been," said Holmes, as he heaved the section of flooring away from the hole. "Hello! What was that?"

We were startled by a knock on the door. "Who's there?" cried Holmes as we both turned. The door had been ajar and now it swung open to reveal Inspector Lestrade.

Holmes." he said, in an offhand manner, "I believe I left my hat here."

"You did not arrive with a hat."

The inspector smiled. "You're right. I did not. But I told the Director I did. Let me get to the point. I have known your methods too long, Holmes, not to suppose that you now own the *Mona Lisa*."

"I make no comment," replied my friend.

"Do you think it really belongs to you, Holmes?"

"Does it not?"

"I should say it belongs to the Louvre."

"Then let me ask you a question. Do you suppose, Lestrade, that the Yard ever told me that Vernet's copy of the *Mona Lisa* was removed from Ryder's House after his death?"

"We are not bound to tell private citizens of all our activities, Holmes."

"You admit I did not know?"

"Yes," he said with a sigh, "I'll admit you didn't know we removed it, if that makes you feel better."

"Much better, thank you. I'm sure you would find British probate law an interesting study, Lestrade. You should know that Watson, here, is a witness to several facts: that the two of us were at Mrs. Ryder's house, that a Mr. Horace proclaimed this painting here a forgery, and that I bought it under the assumption that it was Vernet's copy. I believe that means that the *Mona Lisa*, a stolen painting, was nevertheless bought by me in ignorance. I have a bill of sale from Horace & Horace should you care to see it."

The inspector frowned. "That won't be necessary."

"Good day to you, then, Lestrade. When the Director asks you about your hat, you can tell him you were mistaken about that, too."

The inspector gave a grunt and departed from us in an ill humor.

"Sometimes the official police need to know their boundaries, Watson," said my friend as he unwrapped the painting and hung it above the pine mantle. "Upon further consideration I think I will leave the painting out of its dusty storage for now. After all, I really don't know how long I shall be able to keep it."

"I assume you will carry out Ryder's last wish about returning the *Mona Lisa* to the Louvre?"

"Yes, but not just yet. This case has been a trying one, Watson, and I wish to have some temporary memento of its success. I also want to savor this moment long enough to wash away the memory of my failure in the Nguyen-Kowell dispute. I think I will keep the painting hanging where I can see it until these next eighteen months have passed, or until the probable event within that time of my cousin Peter marrying Miss Ryder."

"What makes you think these two are getting along, Holmes?"

"Only once before have I seen the same wistful look in a cousin that I saw in Peter the day he asked Miss Ryder to paint her portrait, and that when I chanced to be with Peter's older brother, Robert, the day he met the woman whom he shortly afterward married. So I sense that Peter and Rachel Ryder have a future together, and I anticipate a wedding. If I am right, I will give Miss Ryder what I suppose her father would have given her as a sublime gift—a painting by her favorite artist. And I cannot think of a better choice than Vernet's own copy of the *Mona Lisa*. And Vernet, too, will be pleased when I tell him what I paid for it. He will always carry with him the knowledge that someone, in this one instant, at least, was willing to buy one of his paintings for a value exactly equal to the *Mona Lisa*."

"A distinct touch, Holmes," I remarked, as I gazed upon the features of the painting. "I'm beginning to understand what you mean by the painting's superior composition and subtle chiaroscuro. Its primary and secondary foci are certainly balanced admirably. The whole effect is effervescence sprung from the panel, rich in theme and in execution, rich in Nature and in Man, don't you agree?"

Holmes made no immediate reply but seemed lost in thought. "I think," stammered Holmes after some minutes of continual gaze as he marveled in wonder at the painting before him, "it is such a wonderful picture."

Epilogue

Despite his love of da Vinci's masterpiece Sherlock Holmes was not destined to enjoy it for very long. Yet, I do not think he minded, for I was present with him when he removed the painting that held it above the fireplace in Baker Street where he had brought it for the winter. He expressed pleasure that his cousin, though determined to marry, had at least made as wise a choice as he could in the form of Miss Rachel Ryder, whom he believed was an intelligent, fair-minded, and observant woman. It was among the only weddings he ever attended, and I recall one stirring moment when the groom rose to his feet and toasted Holmes with a few short but very moving remarks that left the deepest impression on all those present.

"Holmes, there is a small notice in the *St. James* about Mrs. Ryder," said I, after we had returned from the church wedding that day.

"Just read it to me, Watson."

"I was certain it was here. Wait a minute—ah, yes—:

> *'The public is indebted to Mrs. Elisabeth Ryder of 12 Menard Street for her generous gift to the city of London. Though bereft of her late husband and cousin within the same week of April last (the latter being lost*

on the Titanic) the brave Mrs. Ryder has not allowed her personal sorrows to interfere with the business of charity. A figure rumored to be in the middle four figures has been put into a non-revocable trust in her late husband's name to help the city's poor. Mrs. Ryder's husband was J. Leslie Ryder, the well-known painter. Her cousin, Mr. Wolfgang Kern, was a promoter of art.

The common man of England can be proud that his country is able to produce such selfless persons of philanthropic bent. It is expected that Mrs. Ryder's example will inspire others toward similar acts of beneficence.'"

Holmes remained silent but acknowledged the fact with a slight nod, and though I didn't press him upon the matter I could see he was not displeased.

As to the final details regarding the return of the *Mona Lisa* to its original place in the Salon Carré of the Louvre Museum, Sherlock Holmes made one concession. Director Bantok had retired in autumn, but within a week he experienced a major bout of heart failure, and Vernet learned that the Director's wife was giving her husband what succor she could in his invalid state. Holmes was told of these events and discreetly dropped his demand for a one-line announcement. Still, another year passed before the *Mona Lisa* was finally 'found'. Again, Vernet gave us the details. Sadly, a political struggle among the officials of the Louvre had developed into a furor of disagreement over how monies should be allocated, and a tug-of-war over the cost of a ceremonial return of the *Mona Lisa* was the pivotal issue. The argument raged on until Holmes sent word that his agreement guaranteed that the Louvre would give the public access to the *Mona Lisa* by the fall of 1913, and that if the Museum could not arrange for its unveiling, then he would resume the painting's ownership. This hastened an agreement among the officials, and another plan to explain the painting's recovery, much inferior to Wolfgang Kern's plan, was put into motion as a blind to cover the bickering delay at the Museum. An Italian workman, Vincenzo Perugia, agreed to pose as the luckless thief who had been jealous that the French had acquired the Italian masterpiece. He was secretly promised that his family would receive three thousand lire from an agent of the Louvre for each year he was imprisoned. Perugia was found guilty in July of 1914 and was released immediately, having already served his sentence of seven months in a Florentine jail. Much to Holmes's surprise, the public never questioned the preposterous idea that Perugia, two years after stealing the *Mona Lisa*, would of his own accord write a letter and confess to an Italian curator that he possessed the painting.

"I shall never again underestimate the public's desire to believe fairy tales, Watson," said Holmes, as he bemoaned how the Louvre had duped the public with a plan of recovering the *Mona Lisa* that was so obviously contrived. "Where is imagination and creativity in all this? Where is the artist? Where is the man of the hour, here or anywhere, who stands apart in his genius? We never hear of him anymore. We never see him." Holmes stared moodily at the burning logs upon the iron grate.

I kept silent, but his words stirred within me, and I looked steadfastly in wonder at Holmes. His profile was in shadow as he sat with his legs stretched out before the fire. His violin was in its corner of the room, and the leather pouch with the Italian marbles hung from a nail on the mantle. A small cabinet photo of his cousin and his wife, Rachel Vernet, graced the corner of the desk where I sat. I pondered the whole set of strange circumstances surrounding J. Leslie Ryder, and thought again on that one person Fate thrust into that Gordian mystery to demand its disentanglement—the one man who was creative, imaginative, and genius enough to solve it. All these thoughts were before me as I reached for my inkwell from inside the drawer and laid it upon the desk. I beheld once more that inscrutable figure before the fire. Then I placed a sheet of paper before me and took up my pen.

FINIS